I0651612

Barbara M. Macandrew

Ezekiel

And Other Poems

Barbara M. Macandrew

Ezekiel
And Other Poems

ISBN/EAN: 9783337158194

Printed in Europe, USA, Canada, Australia, Japan

Cover: Foto ©Andreas Hilbeck / pixelio.de

More available books at **www.hansebooks.com**

EZEKIEL

AND

Other Poems.

By B. M.

London:

T. NELSON AND SONS, PATERNOSTER ROW.

EDINBURGH; AND NEW YORK.

1888.

Contents.

EZEKIEL.

'' Also the word of the Lord came unto me, saying, Son of man, behold I take away from thee the desire of thine eyes with a stroke; yet neither shalt thou mourn nor weep, neither shall thy tears run down: forbear to cry, make no mourning for the dead. So I spake to the people in the morning and at even my wife died."

HE knew my soul, He knew she was in truth
   My heart's desire ; and I had none on earth
   But only her.   Upon my troubled life
   She gently shone, as shineth some fair star
   Upon tempestuous waters, as this night
Upon the swellings dark of Jordan shines
The Summer-Moon.
                  Until she rose on me
Earth had no brightness ; for when visions dread
Of God's unutterable glory swept
Before mine eyes, they left me dazzled so
That the sweet, common smiles of moon and sun,
Which gladden other men, grew faint and wan.
And faded in my sky, and served no more

To light mine exile-land. I could not grieve
That earthly things were grown so poor and dark
To eyes which had beheld the Face that shines
Beyond the Sun : I magnify *His* Light,
And my dread office. I would choose to see
The brightness of the heavenly things, although
Their lightning-glory leave me blind henceforth
To any earthly glow : and I would hear
But once the voice of God Almighty sweep
In thunder from His throne, although from hence
Mine ear be deaf to the sweet trembling chime
Of this world's music. I had rather stand
A Prophet of my God, with all the thrills
Of trembling, which must shake the heart of one
Who, in earth's garments, in the vesture frail
Of flesh and blood, is called to minister
As Seraphs do with fire—than bear the palm
Of any other triumph. This my joy
The Lord fulfilled. But when the door would close
In heaven, gathering all the glory in
Of sight and sound, and leaving me alone
Without the Gate to face the darkened earth,
And hear its moan, my soul would mourn to tear
Her earthly vesture, and to clothe herself
With immortality, and so to pass
Within the gates of Light, to stand thenceforth

Among the Sons of God, and minister
Close by the burning Throne.   But God, who willed
That I should tarry here a little while
In the dim outer courts, and speak His word
To many nations, sent me that one star
Of earthly love, that I might be content
To stay a while ; that I might have one sweet,
Sweet tie to earth, to hold my eager soul
A little from the heavenly things, which wooed
With burning glances, till they well-nigh drew
My spirit through the Gates.
                              It was a time
Of tumult and reproach, when God, who clothed
My soul with thunders, bade me utter them
To all the people, whether they would hear
Or would forbear.   When I who stood between
An angry God and angry nations, felt
The shock of their dread warfare, till my soul
Reeled with the clangour—then *she* came to me,
Walking in white, and bearing in her hand
A cup of blessing.   As the waters cool
Which flow from Lebanon, to meet the hot
And thirsty valleys, so she came to me ;
And from that day she was my heart's delight
And comfort for a while, a little while,—
Until God took her.

Oftentimes I came,
With burning thoughts, and with a weary heart,
Towards our little home at eventide,
After a day of conflict.   Then she came
To meet me smiling, and mine eyes would grow
Most sweetly dim, and lose the dazzling Light
Of things unspeakable, and only see
That smile instead.   And she would comfort me,
And sit beside me while the golden sun
Went down in peace, and sweetly sing to me
Some of the songs of Zion.   We were bound
In exile, and we could not sing when those
Who bound us bade us sing the sacred songs
Of the belovèd Land : but when the hour
Of twilight came, when we might rest in peace
Alone together, while the daylight waned,
And the broad shadow of God's wing was spread
Over the exile-hearts, until we seemed
Once more to dwell at home, the captive maids
Of Israël would sing.   They took their harps
At sunset from the willows, and the songs
Were strangely sweet that floated through the land,
Although the sound of Babel's sighing streams
Made mournful answer.

                    Thus she sang to me,
And at the evening-time God gave us light

In our poor dwelling. To *her* gentle eyes
No heavenly doors were opened, she had seen
No glorious visions ; yet she seemed to dwell
More near to God, to hold His name more dear,
And hail Him "Father" with a sweeter trust
Than I, who had beheld in visions dread
The billows of tempestuous glory sweep
Around His throne. But in those evening hours
By the faint starlight, while she sang to me,
My heart grew sweet and calm, and I could rest
With her in God.
    And she was my delight
And comfort for a while, a little while,
Until God called her.

   *   *   *   *   *

     "Son of man, behold,
I take from thee this day thine only one,
Thine heart's desire !"
      He met me in the way,
And thus he smote me. I was going forth,
As I had gone at other times, to speak
His word unto my people : she who was
In truth mine only one, had come with me
Through the bright vineyards. All the leaves were
  stirred
By gentle breezes, all the hills shone clear,

Swept by the morning sunshine, and the birds
Were singing gladly.   At the gate we paused,
That she might turn again, whilst I went forth
Alone to face the people.   That sweet sun
Lighted her gentle face, and whilst I laid
My hand upon her head, I blessed here there
In God's great Name : "The King of Israël,
Whose smile in sunshine brightens all the lands
This summer morn, be with thee evermore
And shine upon thee with His lifted Face,
And comfort thee, as thou dost comfort me,
With tender love.   I bless His Name this day
For His sweet gift to me."   Then, as she went,
I stood to watch her, that no evil thing
Might touch my stainless one, until she reached
Our little exile-home.   In that same hour
God met me with His sword.   "Behold," he said,
" I take from thee this day thine only one,
Thine heart's desire."   Where I had stood and
        prayed
In that calm sunlight, lifting up mine eyes
To the bright Home of God, while Heaven and
        Earth
Seemed full of light and peace, and she had bent
To hear my blessing,—God came straightway
        down,

And said for answer, speaking in His strength,
" I *smite* her ; I will cut her off this day
As with a sword."

    *   *   *   *   *

            Yet I went on my way,
And spake unto the people, for the hand
Of God was strong upon me.   In my heart
The arrow quivered, for the Archer dread
Had driven home His bolt.   I knew that He
Would do as He had said, and take from me
My joy that day.   And every pleasant look
Of earth and sky did smite me ; ah ! how soon
That gentle face would lie close hid from me
By the soft smiling earth, and her fair soul
Walk forth in white beyond that smiling sky
Where I could never see her :—Gentle face
And gentle soul both hidden, and my life
Made desolate.   And yet I spake His word
Who thus had pierced me : yea, I held my soul
From mourning, as a strong man holdeth back
His steed, upon the sudden brink of some
Wild dark abyss.   In the sweet summer-time
Of flowers and sunshine such a gulf of death
And desolation suddenly had yawned
Close at my feet ; yet on the brink I reined
My startled soul, and on the brink I paused

To speak for God,—with such strange calm as God
Can give to dying men, or men with hearts
More dark than death could make them.   What
     although
Ere night mine only joy shall shattered lie
In darkness with the dead?—I must not fail
Nor be discouraged.   In the work of God
No man may turn or falter: I am His,
Not mine, not *hers;* I dare not weep for her
When God hath need of me.   I dare not mourn
The while I speak His word, for no weak tears
May fall upon the sacred fire ; no sound
Of breaking human heart may mar the full
Majestic music of a Prophet's voice,
Speaking to all the ages, from the mount
Of cloud and vision.   Thus I spake for God
And did not falter, rather did my soul
Wax stronger as it overcame.   And still
The hand of God was on me, and I went
From strength to strength, till all the people bent
Before the mighty Word, and many fell
With trembling to the earth.

                              But *once* before,
When I was heralding the things to come
Upon the Holy Place, thus mighty grew
The word of God in me and did prevail :—

When to the Princes in the Gate I spake
At His command, the thunder of His power
Broke on the word, and rose, till, overcome
By that dread sound of wrath, a mighty Prince
Fell at my feet and died.*   Thus have I felt
My soul grow strong, when on the threshold dark
Of some great Vision, the Archangel sounds
The Trump of God.   For while the Trumpet
      peals
In the thick darkness, sounding on and on,
And waxing louder, all my heart is stirred
With new and heavenly powers, till nothing seems
Impossible to me.   Thus rose the word
Of God upon my soul that dreadful day,
And thus I spake it.
                        Then I took my way
Forth from the trembling crowd.   I know my
      brow
Was deadly pale, and as I went mine eyes
Could scarcely see the path.   Deep in my heart
The arrow quivered now.   My thoughts had flown
Again to her, who but once more would come
To meet me smiling.   But the people said,—
" The man of God has stayed himself on God,
Till he can dare all things ; yet even he

Ezekiel xi. 13.

2

Is shaken by the thunder, which he brings
From God to man." I held my way until
I stood in a waste, desert place alone
In the bright afternoon. All things looked strange
And hard to me. By the great lonely stone
Where the Chaldeans worship, when the stars
Snow clear in Heaven, I stayed my steps a while
And looked around me. At no other time
Would I have halted there.

      Yet there I bent
My head at last, and there I hid my face
In my dark mantle. Over me there swept
The winds of desolation.

   *   *   *   *   *

      Once again,
For the last time, we sat at even-tide
Beside the door, and saw the setting sun
Throw on the trembling palm-trees and the streams
His golden showers of light. In days to come
With equal pomp and glory he shall ride
Down all the kindling west, in kingly robes
Of gold and crimson, but *we* shall not watch
His going down. Ah, never more shall scene
On earth be bright to me ;—and as for her,
She hasteth to a land that hath no need
Of changing sun and moon. I hold her close

With my strong arm, but she will find a way
To pass from me to God.   Who ever heard
That *He* could woo in vain ?   What He desires,
That doeth He.
               And she had sung to me
Her last sweet song,—for she was strangely calm
And lifted up.   She did not weep, nor lean
On me, as she had done at other times,
For strength to bear His will ; she seemed to lean
Immediately upon the arm of God,
And need no other aid.   But in that hour
My strength gave way : the gentle voice that sang
Its last, last song so sweetly, seemed to steal
My manhood from me ; and the wistful smile
That strove to comfort me,—the smile so soon
To be eclipsed in death,—did pierce my soul
As with a sword.
            " It is not hard to die,"
She said, with that fair smile, " for God's sweet will
Makes bitter things most sweet.   In my bright
      youth
He calls me to His side.   It is not hard
To go to Him."   But in my haste I said,
With aching heart,—" It is not hard for *thee*—
I know it well.   The captive-exile hastes
To leave the exile-land.   But it is hard

To stay behind alone, when our one star
Is quenched for ever.   Morn or eve shall bring
No word of thee to me, and days and nights
Shall make one empty night."

                    She took my hand
In hers with tender pity, praying God
To comfort me for her :—" And thou must smile
Once more on me, and bid me go in peace
To Him who calls me ; for my short, sweet day
Is closing now, and He would have me Home :
I cannot take that anguished look to wear
On my calm heart in Heaven, as my last,
Last memory of thee until we meet :
Nay, thou must smile on me ; one little smile,
Cast like a wild-flower on my misty way,
Will make it brighter, and I cannot go
In peace until thou bless me."

                    Then she looked
From me to the faint hills, that distant shone
Towards the sinking sun.   And I could feel
That, as she moved a little in my arms,
Her soul was stirring gently, as a bird
Stirs in its nest, about to take its flight
To brighter lands.   And from her eyes the veil
Was falling ; things unspeakable and sweet
Were dawning on her gaze.   In that last hour

The Hosts of God were round us, and *her* eyes
Beheld them, while from mine the dark, sad wing
Of Azrael had hid all brighter things.
I only saw that tender, changing face,
With its most wistful smile :—" She shall not go
From me to follow Thee ! For she is mine,
My fair white lamb, mine only one ; whilst Thou
Hast many, in Thy calm Fold on the hill
Of frankincense and myrrh. Lord, be content
To lead Thy flock where shining waters sleep ;
And leave the poor man in the wilderness
His one ewe lamb !"
            But yet again she said,
Appealing to me, " Suffer me to go
To Him who calleth me ! I love thee so
That none but He could woo me from thy side,
Or make my heart content to go from thee
To all the joys of Heaven. And from the walls
Of that bright Palace-Home my soul will lean,
At morn and eve, to catch some distant sound
Of thy home-coming feet : as here I watched
For thy return at eve.
            " If God had willed,
I would have gladly stayed ; but we are His,
And it is sweet to do a little thing
For Him who loves us so. He needeth me

To be a sign for Him,—my death to stand
A figure to my people, of the things
Which He will do on them, except they turn
And seek His face.   And I am so content
To die for this !   I could not speak for God,
As thou hast done so well ; but I can die
For God, and for my people,—and for *thee*—
To aid in thy great work.

                        " Forbid me not ;
Deny me not to Him.   A day shall come
When He shall give His Dearest to the death,
For thee and me !"   The clouds had parted
    now,
The love of God was shed abroad, within
My broken heart.   I could not say Him, Nay ;
Or question Him.   I laid my sacrifice
Upon His altar, not denying Him
Mine only one.

                  The stars came forth to crown
The sad, still Night.   I heard the distant song
Of one who sang, down by the river-side,
A song of Zion.   From our exile-land
My love was hastening, to the brighter Home
Of Israël.   I bent to kiss her cheek,
And blessed her softly in the Name of God,
And bade her go in peace.   Yea, with a smile

Which God had given me, I loosed my hold
And suffered her to rise and go to Him.

    *   *   *   *   *

And now at evening-time, when all the stars
Keep watch along the battlements of Heaven,
She bendeth from the Palace-walls, to watch
For my Home-going step.
                I must fulfil
My stormy day : once more the clouds of God
Do compass all my path, with visions dread
Of gloom and glory.   By my ruined home
I stand to speak for God, and stretch my hands,
Emptied of their sweet treasure, in God's name
To all the people.   And the Lord alone
Himself doth comfort me.
              And when at length
The evening-time of my long day shall come,
And God shall give me leave to lay aside
The Prophet's mournful mantle, for the robe
Of joy and light,—when at His Gate I find
An everlasting entrance, there my love
Shall meet me smiling.   After my long day
Of storm and conflict, I shall feel once more
The joy of finding her awaiting me
At eventide, and drawing me to rest
With her in God.   Then shall I hear at length

Her sweet voice singing to the harps of gold,
And see her crowned with joy.

                  And He of whom
She spake to me that night, the Son of God,
The saving King of Israël, shall dwell
With us, and be our God.

COMING.

" At even, or at midnight, or at the cock-crowing, or in the morning."

"T may be in the evening,
    When the work of the day is done,
  And you have time to sit in the twilight
    And watch the sinking sun,
  While the long bright day dies slowly
    Over the sea,
And the hour grows quiet and holy
    With thoughts of Me ;
While you hear the village children
    Passing along the street,
Among those thronging footsteps
    May come the sound of *My* feet :
Therefore I tell you, Watch
    By the light of the evening star,
When the room is growing dusky
    As the clouds afar ;

Let the door be on the latch
       In your home,
For it may be through the gloaming
       I will come.

" It may be when the midnight
       Is heavy upon the land,
And the black waves lying dumbly
       Along the sand ;
When the moonless night draws close,
And the lights are out in the house ;
When the fires burn low and red,
And the watch is ticking loudly
       Beside the bed :
Though you sleep, tired out, on your
              couch,
Still your heart must wake and watch
       In the dark room,
For it may be that at midnight
       I will come.

" It may be at the cock-crow,
When the night is dying slowly
       In the sky,
And the sea looks calm and holy,
       Waiting for the dawn

Of the golden sun,
  Which draweth nigh ;
When the mists are on the valleys, shading
  The rivers chill,
And My morning-star is fading, fading
  Over the hill :
Behold, I say unto you, Watch ;
Let the door be on the latch
  In your home ;
In the chill before the dawning,
Between the night and morning,
  I may come.

" It may be in the morning,
    When the sun is bright and strong,
  And the dew is glittering sharply
    Over the little lawn ;
  When the waves are laughing loudly
    Along the shore,
  And the little birds are singing sweetly
    About the door ;
  With the long day's work before you,
    You rise up with the sun,
  And the neighbours come in to talk a
      little
    Of all that must be done ;

But remember that *I* may be the next
    To come in at the door,
To call you from all your busy work
    For evermore :
As you work your heart must watch,
For the door is on the latch
    In your room,
And it may be in the morning
    I will come."

So He passed down my cottage garden,
    By the path that leads to the sea,
Till He came to the turn of the little road
    Where the birch and laburnum tree
    Lean over and arch the way ;
    There I saw Him a moment stay,
And turn once more to me,
    As I wept at the cottage door,
And lift up his hands in blessing—
    Then I saw His face no more.

And I stood still in the doorway,
    Leaning against the wall,
Not heeding the fair white roses,
    Though I crushed them and let them
      fall ;

Only looking down the pathway,
    And looking towards the sea,
And wondering, and wondering
    When He would come back for me,
Till I was aware of an Angel
    Who was going swiftly by,
With the gladness of one who goeth
    In the light of God Most High.
He passed the end of the cottage
    Towards the garden gate,—
(I suppose he was come down
At the setting of the sun
To comfort some one in the village
    Whose dwelling was desolate),
And he paused before the door
    Beside my place,
And the likeness of a smile
    Was on his face :—
" Weep not," he said, " for unto you is given
    To watch for the coming of His feet
Who is the Glory of our blessed Heaven ;
    The work and watching will be very
        sweet
    Even in an earthly home,
And in such an hour as you think not
    He will come."

So I am watching quietly
    Every day.
Whenever the sun shines brightly
    I rise and say,—
" Surely it is tne shining of His face,"
And look unto the gates of His high place
    Beyond the sea,
For I know He is coming shortly
    To summon me.
And when a shadow falls across the window
    Of my room,
Where I am working my appointed task,
I lift my head to watch the door, and ask
    If He is come ;
And the Angel answers sweetly
    In my home,—
" Only a few more shadows,
    And He will come."

THE NIGHT SERVICE.

" Behold, bless ye the Lord, all ye servants of the Lord, which by night stand
in the house of the Lord."

FROM the awaking of the glorious Sun
  In the far chambers of the crystal East,
  To where he goeth down in pomp and power
  Beyond the western seas, the Name of God
  Is to be blessed and praised.

                              In morning hours,
When the sweet singing voice of birds is heard
On every side, when mighty Forests wake
And stretch their hands to God, when through the
    Earth
The breath of Life is blowing,—then the Saints
Arise from sleep and sing.

                      Through all the hours
Of night and darkness, angel-hosts have kept

Their sacred watch, encamping tenderly
Round God's belovèd.   When the curtains rise
At break of day, and show the dewy Earth
Sparkling with heavenly smiles, and wearing crowns
Of peace and beauty undefiled by man,
We marvel at the radiance of her look.
We need not marvel ; she hath entertained,
Whilst we were sleeping, angel-guests as fair
As stars of the morning.   When her children sleep—
Their sad eyes closed, their weary feet that are
So restless all the day, and vex her with
Their ceaseless wanderings, lying very still
Upon her bosom, lo ! the far-off Gates
Of Glory lift their heads, the hosts of God
Descend to visit her.

                    Ah ! Night is sweet
With fragrance of eternal lilies, worn
On stainless breasts.   And wonderful deep thrill
Of heavenly music come and go, on wings
Of the midnight wind, and wander tenderly
On sleeping seas.

                        From darkened shore to shore
God gives his children sleep—their faces pale
And mournful, overshone by angel-looks

That light their dreams. And when the morning
    breaks
And rouses them from sleep, they rise and sing
For joy of heart. Their sleep has been most sweet
And full of peace ; the saddest face has caught
Some faint reflection from an angel's smile ;
And the soft wind that bloweth from the East
At daybreak, finds upon the dewy heath
Some trace of footsteps, fragrant from the Hills
Of Frankincense and Myrrh. Oh, sweetly rise
Our morning-songs to God, in whose great Light
We see the light.

           And through the long bright Day
There is no silence, for at every hour
Some soul is praising God. A mighty man
Standing victorious, after desperate fight
Upon his Battle-field—his high soul thrilled
With awful triumph, and his gleaming eyes
Still full of stormy light—uplifteth now
His mailèd hands to Heaven, and blesseth God,
The God of Battles. Now a woman, pale
With nights of weeping, veiling her in clouds
Of shadowy hair, and wearing for a smile
A sadder light than moonlight on her face,
Steals to the Saviour's feet, and poureth there

3

Her most sweet ointment, till the House is filled ·
With heavenly fragrance.   Now a little child
Of the kingdom raises his sweet voice to sing
A song of Zion—no deep undertone
Of the Battle's thunder past, no voice of tears,
Sound in the simple song ; his sky is bright,
His full cup runneth over, and he sings.
Thus every hour some soul is giving praise,
Sweet praise, to God.   The mighty man of war
In a deep, grand hymn, sung with a voice still hoarse
After the Battle-shout ; a woman's kiss
Falling, with tears of trembling joy, on Feet
Most sacred ; and the sweet voice of a child
Singing between : these make the music heard
On high.

   But who shall praise God in the Night ?
The Night, that lays her finger on the lips
Of men, and hushes them to something like
The calm of Death.   How sleeps the prisoner,
And the oppressor sleeps ; the wicked cease
From troubling, and the weary are at rest.
Ah, who shall praise Him in the Night ? the
  Night,
That stretcheth mournful wings from shore to ·
  shore,

Till silent lie the singers of the world
Beneath the shadow.

Angels come and go,
And wonderful sweet thrills of music sweep
The night-wind as they pass. Yea, Christ Himself
Is with us; lo! the Shepherd-king of the Church
Abideth in the Fields, and watcheth o'er
His Flock by night. But who shall give Him praise
For this sweet service? Who shall celebrate
The Name of God by Night.

It *is* the Night:
And in the Temple of the Lord, not made
By mortal hands, the lights are burning low
Before the Altar. Clouds of darkness fill
The vastness of the sacred aisles. The dumb
And breathless Spirit of the Night is here
In all his power; no rushing mighty wind
Of organ-harmonies is sweeping down
The shadowy place. A few short hours ago,
And all the Temple-courts were thronged with those
Who worshipped and gave thanks, before they went
To take their rest. Then many voices joined
To sing the praise of God; but who shall bless
His Name at midnight?

                Lo! a band of pale
Yet joyful priests do minister around
The Altar, where the lights are burning low,
In the breathless Night. Each grave brow wears the
    crown
Of sorrow, and each heart is kept awake
By its own restless pain, for these are they
To whom the night-watch is appointed. See!
They lift their hands, and bless God in the Night!
Whilst we are sleeping, those to whom the King
Has measured out a cup of sorrow, sweet
With His dear love, yet very hard to drink,
Are waking in His Temple, and the eyes
That cannot sleep for sorrow or for pain
Are lifted up to Heaven; and sweet low songs,
Broken by patient tears, arise to God.
Bless ye the Lord, ye servants of the Lord,
Which stand by Night within His Holy Place
To give Him worship! Ye are Priests to Him,
And minister around the Altar, pale
Yet joyful in the Night.

                The Priests must serve,
Each in his course, and *we* must stand in turn
Awake with sorrow, in the Temple dim,
To bless the Lord by Night. We will not fear

When we are called at midnight, by some stroke
Of sudden pain, to rise and minister
Before the Lord.   We, too, will bless His Name
In the solemn Night, and stretch our hands to Him.

THE MAN AT THE GATE.*

"' I am willing, with all my heart,' said He."—*Bunyan's Pilgrim's Progress*

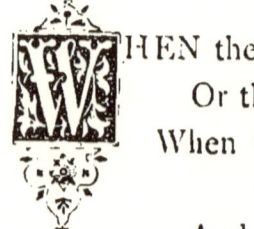HEN the sun shines fair on the smiling land,
 Or the stars walk out in a cloudless sky,—
When the waves are trampling wild on the
  sand,
 And the voice of the thunder passes by,—

In summer and winter, in calm and storm,
 When the morning dawns, and the night falls late,
We may catch, if we will, the steadfast form
 Of the Man that watches beside the Gate.

In the early spring, when the voice was heard
 Of the singing birds in their sweet defiles,
When the face of the earth once more was stirred
 By the flowers that came and went like smiles,

* Written for a Sunday afternoon class, in connection with a lesson from the "Pilgrim's Progress."

I saw the stars of the morning wait
  On their lofty towers to watch the land,
As a little child stole up to the Gate,
  And knocked with a tiny trembling hand ;

A wreath of flowers on his golden hair,
  The light of youth in his shining eyes,
And the look of an earnest purpose there,
  As of one who must win a place in the skies,—

" I am only a little child, dear Lord,
  And my feet are stained already with sin,
But they said you had sent the children word
  To come to the Gate and enter in."

The Man at the Gate looked up and smiled,
  A heavenly smile, and fair to see,
And He opened, and bent to the pleading child,—
  " I am willing, with all My heart," said He.

The morning breaks, with its golden showers,
  The pale stars pass away to their rest,
As the little head with its wreath of flowers
  Is laid on the Shepherd's gentle breast ;

While over it bends in speechless love
  The Head that is crowned with thorns for him ;
Ah, the angels might sigh in their songs above
  For the tears that are making the child's eye dim.

     *   *   *   *   *

I looked again, and the wintry blast
  Was hurrying wildly o'er land and sea,
The glory of spring-time was long gone past,
  And the branches were bare on the trembling tree.

Yet still at the Gate the Saviour stood,
  And His Face was uplifted serene and fair,
Though His raiment was heavy and red with blood,
  And the crown of thorns showed dark on His hair

It was afternoon, and the sun was low,
  And the troubled winds sobbed long and loud,
As an old man tottered across the snow,
  Which wrapt the earth in a bitter shroud ;

He knocked with a withered, trembling hand :
  " I can but perish at last," he said,
" For the cruel night comes fast on the land,
  And the morning will find me cold and dead.

" O Thou that watchest beside the Gate,
    Had I come to Thee in the days gone by
Thou hadst received me ; but now too late,
    I lay me down on Thy threshold to die :

" I have fought and finished an evil fight,
    I have earned the deadly wages of sin ;
It is hard to die in the snow to-night,
    But no man is willing to take me in."

The sun was low in the changing west,
    The shadows were heavy from hill and tree,
As the Watchman opened the Gate of rest,---
    "*I* am willing, with all My heart," said He.

    *   *   *   *   *

" O gentle Watchman ! turn Thee now
    To rest a while in the House of God ;
Forget the heavy burdens which bow
    The weary of heart in our sad abode :

" Be it far from Thee to watch all night
    For the children of sorrow, and sin, and shame ;
In the heavenly places the lamps are bright,
    And the saints are rising to sing Thy name."

But the Watchman turned and looked on me.
    Till I bent my head adown to weep ;
" Suffer me then to watch with Thee
    Alone to-night while the nations sleep !"

So I watched with Him through the moonless hours
    Of that sweetest night I have ever known,
And His words were as dew on the tender flowers,
    And all in the darkness the true Light shone.

We heard the gentle steps of the snow
    Coming down from its home at God's right hand,
As the angels came softly, long ago,
    To the fragrant hills of the Holy Land.

And at midnight there came the voice of one
    Who had crept to the Gate through the blinding
        snow,
And who moaned at the Gate as one undone
    Might moan at the sight of the last dread Woe.

A woman's voice, and it rose and fell
    On the muffled wings of the snowy night,
With a trembling knocking which seemed to tell
    Of one who was chilled and spent outright.

" I wove the crown for the Brow divine,
  I pierced the Hand that was stretched to save,
I dare not pray that the moon may shine
  To show me the prints of the nails I drave ;

" I beat this night on my sinful breast,
  I dare not pray Him to succour me ".......
But the Watchman opened the Gate of rest,—
  " I am willing. with all My heart," said He.

     *   *   *   *   *

Thus day and night they are pressing nigh,
  With tears and sighs, to the heavenly Gate,
Where the Watchman stands in His majesty,
  With a patience which never has said, " Too
    late."

Let the sorrowful children of want and sin
  Draw near to the Gate, whence none depart ;
Let the nations arise and enter in,
  For the Lord is willing, with all His heart.

THE HEBREW MOTHER.

Arise thou therefore, get thee to thine own house ; and when thy feet enter into the city the child shall die."—1 KINGS xiv. 12.

ITHIN our palace-gates another king
Was come to stand, a dim and silent king,
Whom no man seeketh after, and no man
Resisteth, when he riseth up to smite.
  In robes of darkness and with soundless
    tread
He came at midnight, when the moon was full
And all the land was silent ; for I sat
That night to watch the child, and rising up
At midnight, drew the curtains wide to see
The silent skies.   Forth on the palace court
I looked : the scent of the white orange-flowers
Came and went sweetly on the still night air,
The fountain played and murmured in the court,
And fair flowers trembled round it, and the moon
Gleamed on white marble pillars.

Then there fell
A Shadow suddenly, and *one* did stand
In robes of darkness, where the moonlight lay
Most white and shining on the marble floor.
A king—for the dim form as of a crown
Rose on that shrouded head ; an angel too—
For mighty wings did cast their shade athwart
The moonlight on the floor, proclaiming him
One of God's angels, who excel in strength
And do His awful will : and—with a start
Of sudden agony—I caught the gleam—
The deadly gleaming of the sword he held
Wherewith to smite my child.   Lo, this is Death
Come up into our Palace !
                                        Then I fell
With bitter moanings kneeling by the child,
And stretching helpless hands across his breast
To shield him from the angel of the sword
Whom no man can resist.   He lay asleep
Pale in the moonlight, very beautiful,
And fair and still like those white flowers that
      gleamed
In the same moonlight.   Thus I wept and watched
And called upon His Name who is the hope
Of Israel through dark nights and cloudy days.
The long pale moonlit hours went slowly by.

And it was near the dawning when the child
Awoke, with a long sigh, and looked on me.
Where had *he* been, through those still moonlit
        hours,
While I had watched?   His eyes were wearing now
A new deep look, as if some veil were rent,
And he,—with open face beholding,—saw
Things glorious and secret, and his voice
Thrilled on my heart, and held me calm and still:
"Mother, dear mother, I have loved the Name
Of the great God of Israel, now I go
To see His face.   His blessing on my heart
Is gathering ever, and He draws so close
And shines so sweetly with His peace on me
That I must rise and go.
                              How often we
Have wandered on the glowing sunset hills
Of Ephraim; and at the sacred hour
Of the great evening-sacrifice afar
In Zion, we have knelt towards her gates—
Her holy gates—and prayed the Lord that He
Would reckon *us* among the people there.
And in His holy Temple God did hear
The far-off prayer, which echoed from the hills
Of Ephraim, and on our hearts there fell
(As falls on Israel what time the priest

Comes forth to bless the people) God's own peace
After the sacrifice. This night once more
Strange sweetness seems to fall upon my heart,
As if some one were blessing me with peace
For evermore. This blessing may be *His*—
The High Priest's yet to come—who shall by one
Great Sacrifice, at evening-time, redeem
His people to Himself."
                                The moonlight lay
Upon his face ; but not from moon or star
Had shone the light that dwelt so deep within
Those lifted eyes. Even in the Border Land
The people have no need of sun by day,
Neither of moon by night. These are no more
Their lights, for God Himself is risen up
To be to them an everlasting Light :
And unto Him alone they look, with eyes
Which we must weep to see.
                                He spoke again
In a low tone,—" Dear mother, sing to me
Once more a song of David. I had prayed
To be a king like David, and to reign
For God in Israel, but now I go
To be with David, and with all the great
And mighty men of Israel who stand
Before the Holy One. Dear mother, sing

A song of David." And I sang to him
With bitter thrills of pain ; trembling, and yet
Not weeping, for I knew there would be time
To weep hereafter, but the time was short
Wherein I yet might sing to him, and lay
His head upon my breast.   I sang to him—
Singing the Lord's song, even in the land
Of death and sighing, for the shadows drew
Closer across his face.

                Then, as I ceased,
The king came in to see the child, and bent
To kiss his brow, and bending caught the look
Upon his face, and started,—" This is Death
Come up into our Palace.   O my gods
Whom I have trusted, and to whom my prayers
Have all the night gone up !   Behold, ye turn
Away from me ; now also will I turn
Away from you, and seek unto the Lord
Of Israel and Judah.   Long ago
I used to worship on His holy hill,
And hear the words of peace and blessing fall
On Israel.   But I have sinned, and now—
An angry God—He dwelleth in the Land,
And goeth up and down to smite, and not
To bless, and those who meet Him turn aside
In fear and trembling.   Yet to whom can we

Appeal but Him ! Thou shalt arise and go
To Shiloh, to the man of God, and ask
If yet the child may live.   *I* dare not go,
For I have knelt to other gods than his."

 *   *   *   *

The morning star was smiling sweet and still
In the blue distant sky, what time I rose
To leave my child.   The tears fell silently
And heavy, as I bent my head again,
And yet again, to kiss the cold pale cheek ;—
" How shall I leave thee ?   God Himself be here,
And hold thee back from Death, until I come !
It is a little way : a little while
And I return.   Wait for me till I haste
Across the hills, and come again to thee."
A sweet smile wandered on his fading face,—
" Yes, mother, I will wait ; I shall not come
Again to thee, but thou shalt come to me,
As David said.   It is a little way
Across the hills, and I will wait for thee
With God in Zion."
                          Then I wept again,
And prayed, and turned to go ; perhaps the man
Of God in Shiloh would be strong to save
My dying child.   But at the door again
I turned to look on him.   His eyes were full

4

Of God's own smile, his look was calm and high,
And with his hand he pointed to the star
And smiled,—" *My* star, *my* bright and morning
    star !
The night is ended, and the Day-star come
For me.   And though the darkness on my Land
Shall be for many days, a Star shall rise
On Jacob, and the midnight shadows flee
Before His Face."   And then again he said,
Lifting his hands unto the silent Land
That stretched above his dying head, " My star,
My bright and morning star !"

     *   *   *   *   *

At noontide, when the hot and heavy air
Pressed on the weary earth, and thunder-clouds
Were darkening heaven, and everything was still,
And faint, and sickening with the burning breath
Of coming storms, I stood at length before
The man of God in Shiloh.

                      Then he rose—
That blind and awful Prophet of the Lord—
And stretched his hand to heaven, and the curse
Like thunder burst upon my head from God.
He stretched his hand to heaven, and the clouds
Of heaven answered him, for while he poured
Each awful curse, the thunders crashed above.

And deadly lightnings gleamed and gleamed again.
Curses on Israel, on the pleasant land
Which had been precious in the eyes of God ;
Curses upon her king who had provoked
With many sins that higher King, who reigns
A jealous God in Israel.
                        And still
After each awful curse, the awful crash
Of thunder shook the earth, and smote my heart
As if great voices up in Heaven said
"Amen" to every curse.   And lightnings gleamed,
As if impatient to begin the work
Of judgment in the land.   I fell upon
My face.   I think I would have died before
The Lord that day, what time His thunders woke,
And His blind Prophet in dread words proclaimed
The darkness and the doom of Israel,—
But ever and anon the sweet, child's voice
Which spoke to me at dawning (when there were
No thunders in the sky, but only stars—
Fair morning stars—which seemed to sing once
    more
Together to the Lord), would steal across,
My trembling soul, " *Yet* shall a Star arise
On Jacob, and the midnight shadows flee
Before His Face."   I tried to stay my heart

Upon this word, until amid the crash
Of thunders and of curses, I did hear
His words about the child,—how he should die
That very day in peace, and Israel
Should mourn for him ;—" He shall not live to see
The evil days.   What time thy feet do pass
This day within thy city-gate, the child
Shall die."

     *   *   *   *   *

                     I know not how I went that day
Along the road from Shiloh.   All my heart
Seemed stunned and stricken, as by some wild blow
Dealt by an unseen hand.   I hurried on,
And could not bear to tarry on the road,—
Although I knew that every step I took
In hastening to the child, brought *Death* more
    near—
Not *me* more near—to him.   I know I prayed
At times, not asking anything, I think,
But helplessly repeating God's great Name
In my great agony.   And thus I went
In my strange haste, until I reached the gate
Of Tirzah : on her palaces and towers
The afternoon was shining, and the gate
Stood open.   *Then* it seemed as if a dream,
A woful dream, had wrapped me all the day,—

But the gate woke me, and the word came back
And smote upon me like a blow from God
Given in anger,—" When thy feet do pass
This day within the city-gate, the child
Shall die."
　　　　　　Then my heart fainted utterly,
And all things seemed to darken, and I crept
A little from the gate, and stumbled where
The graves are thickest.　There the people lie
And weep no more ; the stately trees that keep
Their dark watch in the place of graves are
　　　used
To shelter calmer faces, stiller hearts
Than mine.　In their deep shadows I fell down
And tried to call on God, but in that hour
Of agony, the clouds were dark between
My soul and Him ; " O God ! I cannot pass
Within the gate.　Where are Thy mercies gone ?
Would God that I had died for thee, my son !"
　　*　　　　*　　　　*　　　　*　　　　*
But suddenly there was the voice of one
Who spake to me
　　　　　　　　Sweeter than sweetest flow
Of waters which go softly, music swept
Across my heart : the music of a voice
Used to the songs of Heaven.　How that tone,

With its strange sweetness, touched my anguished
    heart
To something more than tears : the fountains then
Of a great deep were broken, and I poured
My heart to God.   (It was of God the voice
Had spoken.)   All the bitterness was gone,
And, like a little child, I leaned my head
Upon my God.   The Angel stood by me,
And smiled, in that dim place of graves, a smile
Which surely even in bright Heaven would
Have seemed exceeding bright ; and yet as soft
As that soft music of his angel-voice,—
" Poor mother ! I am come to take thy hand
And lead thee through the gate, for it is hard
For thee to rise and go.   My God and thine "—
(How sweetly, with the thrill of *perfect* love,
And yet with holy awe, as if he stood
Before the Throne, the Angel named that Name)—
" My God and thine—hath sent me unto thee
To lead thee through the gate."
                          But at the word
My heart grew faint again, and though I tried
To lean on God, trembling took hold on me :
And, with a voice that sounded hoarse and strange
To mine own ear, I answered him again,—
" Within our palace-court the Angel dread

Of Death is standing, and what time I pass
This day within the city-gate, *his* feet
Shall cross the inner threshold, and his sword
Shall smite my child!" But in that dark wild
    hour,—
When my soul fainted almost unto death,—
The Lord did wondrously.

                 A strange bright cloud
Did overshadow us ; and I beheld,
And lo ! a City. Eye hath never seen
On this pale earth such glory, ear hath heard
No music like the songs which seemed to float
Across the place. Above the City stood
No sun, yet forth she looked, clear as the sun,
Fair as the moon, and terrible as some
Great army. And the shining of her walls
Was like the glory of a golden Dawn
On stainless snow. Upon the streets there went
And came a holy people, clad in white,
With faces sealed to peace unspeakable.
I did not see His Face who sitteth King
Within the shining City, but I saw
Reflected on each face His wondrous look,
And I could read that every eye within
The City saw Him, though I saw Him not.
The gates were open, and the voice of them

That sing for joy of heart was heard again
Within.

        The Angel of the Lord stood by,—
Watching, methought, to see what *I* would think
Of this, his blessed Home.   He took my hand
And pointed to the City,—" Beautiful
For situation, joy of all the earth
Is God's fair Zion !   Thou shalt rise and come
(Even with joy) within this dreaded gate
Of Tirzah ; for what time thy weary feet
Do pass across this city-gate, the child
Shall cross *that* Threshold, and behold the Face
Of God in peace."

           Then had I strength to rise,
And,—gazing steadfastly unto that fair
And shining City,—leaning on the hand
Of God's good Angel, passed unto the gate
Of Tirzah.

          Yea, through God, I did prevail
To cross—although with something like the throb
Of Death (for my child's soul was parting then)—
Within the gate.

     *   *   *   *   *

          I lean on God.   My child
Shall see no evil days.   What time I passed
That day within the gate, the child arose

And crossed Thy Threshold, and beheld thy
    Face,
O God, in peace.   He will not come to me.
But I will haste across the fading hills
And go to Thee.

SAVONAROLA.

I.

LOW kneeleth the monk at prayer
    In his desolate cell,
Pale as death his lifted brow,
    His hands are clenched and pale ;
He cannot heed, in this hour of need
    The call of the convent bell

In the cloisters fair without,
    In the moonlight sweet,
May be heard the passing sound
    Of sandalled feet ;
For the monks are risen at dead of night
To pray in the church for grace and light,
    The dim new year to greet :

The voice of the midnight bell,
    On the crystal air,

Hath summoned the men that slept to wake
  And think of prayer ;
As the old year dies, and the curtains rise
  On a strange new year.

But the monk who kneeleth alone
  In his desolate cell,
Is wrapped already in prayer too deep
  To hear the voice of the bell ;
Eight nights hath he watched in agony
  Which none may tell.

His hands are clenched and raised
  In the conflict dread,
His passionate gaze is on the cross
  Above his head ;
On the face of One who hangs thereon,
With piercèd hands and thorny crown,
  Dying or dead.

And scarce more worn and sad
  That awful face,
That leans, in the heaviness of death,
  From its high place,
Than the wasted face upturned to plead
  For strength and grace.

He prayeth low for aid,
   To meet the frown
Of those who shall give him to share
    cross—
   That thorny crown ;
But, voiceless, upon the mournful prayer
   The mournful Christ looks down.

How dreadful is this place !
   A living man in his woe,
And a marble Christ, who never stirs
   Where they nailed him long ago ;
Awfully gazing face to face
   With the anguished soul below.

Fair walketh the moon in heaven
   With her silver tread,
As the sweet saints walk in robes of snow
   In the land of the blessèd dead ;
And she casteth a radiance tender and pale
   Upon the Saviour's head.

The sun grew faint in Heaven
   Before His woe,
But now the moon with her gentle gaze
   Can face Him so ;

Knowing that Christ, from the sorrows of
    death,
Was comforted long ago.

The monk hath turned at length
    To those shining skies,—
"Surely God is not in this place,
    I will arise,
And watch afar till the morning star
    Shall bless mine eyes.

"I turn me from the cross,
    To the Crucified—
Will He strengthen me to tread the path
    His own feet dyed?
Will He look forth from His lattice to-night,
And show me the smile, serene and bright,
    That cheers His bride?

Is the fire that burns in my heart alway
    The fire of God?
Is my voice to bear the awful sound
    Of His wrath abroad?
Saviour divine, show me a sign
    To light my road!"

In that same hour the Lord
   Unveiled His face,
Sending His Spirit down to bless
   The solitary place :
Teaching those weary eyes to see,
No marble Christ in agony,
   But a living King of Grace :

And the King hath laid His hand
   On the watcher's head,
Till the heart that was so worn and sad
   Is quiet and comforted ;
And the soul is strong once more to stand,
And face the wrath of all the land,
   With His message dread.

II.

The people are met to pray
   Before the shrine,
Where day and night, from year to year,
   The pale lamps shine,
To light the darkness of a Face
That bendeth from the altar-place,
   Sad, yet divine.

The clouds of incense rise,
   The sweet bell tolls.
Down all the darkness of the church
   A music rolls,
And stirs, as with a wind from Heaven,
   The gathered souls.

But when the passionate voice
   Of the music dies,
And even the echo, faint and sweet,
   Hath ceased her sighs,
Another voice, more solemn and grand,
   Is heard to rise !

Ah ! well fair Florence knows
   That voice of doom ;*
This is her Prophet. stern and sad
   Whose soul doth loom
So dark and awful from its place,
That they who dare to meet His face
   Pale at its gloom.

How fair and sweet on the hills
   Their footsteps glow,

* " His voice was as the blast of the archangel's trumpet."

Who come with tidings of peace and love
　To the world below ;
As angels of light, by day and night,
　They come and go :

But those whom God has appointed
　Heralds of wrath,
From his secret place of thunder
　Come by a darker path ;
A voice of doom, a brow of gloom,
　This herald hath.

To him the smiles of earth
　Are little worth,
His eyes have seen the lifted sword
　Gleam wild in the north,
And he speaks as one to whom is given
To know the wrath of outraged Heaven,
　And to pour it forth.

Yet are there softer hours,
　When his voice sinks low,
And they see, as it were, an angel's face ;
　So sweet the glow
With which he prays them all to come
To the arms of Christ, who is our home,
　And loveth so.

" I have longed as other men
    To be at rest,
To follow the sinking, smiling sun
    Down the shining west,
Or to take the wings of the morning and flee
    To my Saviour's breast :

" Yet, might I go to Him
    This night in peace,
How could I sing in the silver dawn
    Of that sweet release,
Whilst my people darkly stand without,
And lift to Heaven the rebel shout,
    That will not cease ?

" Oh, that mine eyes were fountains
    Of flowing tears,
That I might weep through the sunless hours
    Of my bitter years;
For my land hath filled her cup of sin,
    And the judgment nears;

Then all the people trembled
    For fear of God,
As if they saw in heaven the sign
    Of His lifted rod,

5

And felt the truth that, a little while,
And instead of the light of His fatherly smile
His wrath should be shed abroad.

III.

They brought him forth to die
In the face of the sun,
They took his sacred robes away
One by one ;
Whilst the city gazed, he stood amazed,
As a man undone.

The lips that were bathed in fire
Are silent and pale,
The marks of tempest and agony,
And of hope that doth fail,
Are on the brow that *was* so high—
It faced God's thund'.rs in the sky,
And could not quail.

Has he missed the cup of joy,
Whose rich wine glows
With heavenly radiance, pourèd forth
For the lips of those
Who dare to face a martyr's death,
A martyr's gathered woes?

Is there no cup for him
    But the cup of agony?
No ecstasy of faith and prayer,
    No parted sky?
Yet, steadfastly he standeth there,
Unaided in his last despair,
    And dares to die.

Within the chambers dark
    Of his wrapt soul,
Strange scenes are passing fitfully,
    Strange voices roll;
He lives again the last dark days,
    Whilst the bell doth toll.

He hears once more the witness
    Of the accusing band:
" Thy words have been bold against the men
    That rule in tne ianu,
Yea. and the Church of God, amazed,
Has heard thy voice in thunder raised
    To blast her hand !"

They said he bore it well—
    The torture dread—

They racked his broken frame again
   From foot to head,
Till the quivering lips denied the truth—
   He knew not what he said !

" When the blood-red mists had cleared
   From my reeling brain,
And the pale daylight that had been lost
   Crept back again,
I looked on the white robe of my soul
   And saw its deadly stain.

" How awfully that stain
   Did grow and gloom,
Even whilst I hastened to speak the words
   That sealed my doom,
Denying the false denial, wrung
From lips to which the cold sweat clung,
   In the torture-room.

" And now they bid me yield
   This weary breath ;
I, who have lost my Saviour's smile
   And shipwrecked faith,
Am still allowed to die for Him,

In my poor raiment, soiled and dim --
A martyr's sacred death.

" Last night I saw God's hosts
    On the moonlight ride,
And as they passed each martyr drew
    His stainless robe aside,
Lest I should seek to touch the hem
    That floated wide.

" *They* died for the love of Christ
    By fire and sword,
And He Himself stood by to cheer
    With smile and word ;
I die, alone, for Him to-day
    My lost, lost Lord ! "

Within the chambers dark
    Of his rapt soul,
Such thoughts were passing drearily
    Whilst the bell did toll,
And sunny Florence smiled to see
Her noblest son, in agony,
    Draw near the goal.

He was aware of a voice
    That cried aloud.

" We blot thy name this day," it said,
    " From the Church of God ;
O homeless soul, the thunders roll
    Along thy downward road !"

But even as it spake—
    Through all the place
A murmur ran, for a nameless change
    Was on the martyr's face,
As if a golden hope, that slept
Deep in his soul, had waked and leapt
    To meet a coming grace.

A glorious gleam of heaven *
    Lighted his eye :
" Ye may blot my name from the Church
      on earth ;
    But the Church of the sky,
Christ's radiant Bride, is opening wide
    The Gates of Victory.

" And I, a man despised,
    Shall enter there

---

* During the ceremony of stripping him of his sacerdotal dress, Savonarola stood gloomy and abstracted; but when the bishop pronounced the words, "I separate thee from the Church," a sudden hope lighted his face, and he answered aloud, "From the Church Militant, but *not* from the Church Triumphant."

Amongst the priests of the House of God,
   Clean and fair,
The clouds are broken overhead,
The smile of Christ's own lips is shed
   On my despair."

No golden dawn that glitters
   On the Eastern sea,
No burning glories of the West
   Which transient be,
Can image how that light broke forth,
   O blessèd martyr, on thee!

He stood transfigured there,
   In the smile of God,
Not noting the fear and wrath that shook
   The cruel crowd,
Not knowing how they set him free,
To stand with Christ in ecstasy,
   Where the angels sang aloud.

THE SEA OF SORROW.

I

T was the Sea of Sorrow : neither sun
  Nor moon did lighten it ; the waters slept,
  And dreamed not as they slept, for smile nor
      frown
  Did cross their face.   Around, the moun-
      tains swept,
Like a great host at rest ; and I beheld
The shadow of Eternity lie deep
And heavy on the sea.

      A sad, chill wind
Did wander by the shore, but never stirred
Those dreamlike waters ; and amongst the dim
Eternal mountains, I could hear the tread
Of solemn thunders.   Common sounds of earth
Were hushed to silence there : the voice of bride
And bridegroom ceased ; the reaper's song of joy,
The victor's cry, died trembling on the hills

That compassed round the sea, and never reached
The sunless face, nor stirred the sunless heart.

II.

It was the Sea of Sorrow ; and I saw
The Master walk thereon.   His robe was dark ;
The crown was on his brow—that mournful crown
Which marked him King of Sorrows : this the gift
Which his fair Earth presented to her Lord
When he did visit her.   For other men
She twineth smilingly her laurel crowns ;
But unto *Him* she offered—woful gift—
A crown of thorns.   Yet he accepted it—
Yea, he desired it, counting it all joy
To wear that piercing gift.
                         And wearing it,
He treadeth, kingly, on the waters dim,
Fairer than sons of men, though under skies
More dark than Earth had seen.   For all things
     seemed
To fight against Him : heaven was black with clouds,
And terrible upon the mountains shone
The feet of hurrying storms, the rapid glance
Of scattered lightnings ; then the thunders loud
Broke on that lonely sea, and on the Man
Who walked thereon ; then met upon His head

The sorrows of eternal death, and none
For whom He died were found to comfort Christ.

III.

It was the Sea of Sorrow ; waters gray
And mournful stretched from solemn shore to shore.
In a dark rest which none may break or mar :
And there once more the Master.   He was dead,
But is alive again, and walketh now
In robes of light across the waters dim,
Leading His chosen band.   These be the men
Who suffer with Him—clad, like Him, in white ;
And more than conquerors, for they can tread
With slow and even step the dreadful plain
Of those deep waters, hasting not for fear
Even in the dreariest night.

                         And there were hours
When strange, unearthly radiance flushed the face
Of those dim waters ; when the City throned
Above the stars looked down upon the sea,
Which caught the glorious image.   Then the men
That walked thereon beheld beneath their feet
The shadow of the Heavenly—walls and towers
Of gems and crystal : as they walked the cold
And deathly waters, lo ! they seemed to tread
The streets of gold above.   For Christ, and those

Who walk with Him in white—where heart and
    flesh
Must well-nigh faint and fail—thus going down
To God's great sea, behold God's wonders there :
And precious things of everlasting grace
And secret glory are revealed to eyes
That mourn the death of every earthly joy.

IV.

It was the Sea of Sorrow ; and I stood
At midnight on the shore. The heavy skies
Hung dark above ; the voice of them that wept
Was heard upon the waters, and the chill,
Sad going of a midnight wind, which stirred
No wave thereon. And I was there alone
To face that dreadful sea : I felt the cold
And deathly waters touch my feet, and drew
A little back, and shuddered. Yet I knew
That all who follow Christ must suffer here.
" Master," I said, with trembling, in the night,
With voice that none but *He* would note or know,
So hoarse and weak—" O Master, bid me come !
If on these woful waters I must walk,
Then let me hear Thy voice thereon, that so
I may not die, before I reach Thy feet,
Of loneliness and fear."

                    I listened there
With breathless longing by that solemn sea,
Till through the curtains of the night I heard
His own voice calling me—that voice which draws
His children through the flood and through the fire
To kiss His feet ; and at the Master's word
I left the shore, forth walking on the dim
And untried waters, there to follow Him
Who callèd me, and there to see His face.

                    v.

It was the Sea of Sorrow.   Ages gray
Had come and gone : and every age had some
Who were accounted worthy to attain
The laurel crowns of earth, and walk in robes
Of purple, far above their brother-men ;
And every age had some whom *God* had called
To walk in white with Christ—to follow One
Who wore a crown of thorns where moonless skies
Bent dark o'er darker seas.
                    A little while,
And all things shall be new ; the night of earth
Shall pass away for ever ; " no more sea "
Shall then be found, for pain and loss and grief
Are swallowed up in radiant victory.
Yet in the country of eternal Spring

Many shall bend to kiss the Master's feet,
Saying,—" He never smiled so sweet before,
Save on the Sea of Sorrow, when the night
Was saddest on our heart.   We followed Him
At other times in sunshine.   Summer days
And moonlight nights He led us over paths
Bordered with pleasant flowers : but when His steps
Were on the mighty waters—when we went
With trembling hearts through nights of pain and loss—
His smile was sweeter and His love more dear ;
And *only* Heaven is better than to walk
With Christ at midnight over moonless seas."

A SONG OF THE RIVER.

ANY waters go softly dreaming
   On to the sea ;
But the River of Death floweth softest
   By tower and tree ;

By smiling village and meadow,
   In the morning light ;
By palace-gate and by cottage,
   In the dim hush of night.

No sigh when the wistful moonlight
   Seeks that cold breast—
No smile when the gold of sunset
   Burns in the west—

No rush of the mournful waters
   Breaks on the ear—
To tell us, when Life is strongest,
   That Death flows near.

But through throbbing hearts of cities,
    In the heat of the day,
The cool dark River passeth
    On its silent way :

And where the Good Shepherd leadeth
    To pastures green,
Ever the dark " still waters"
    Of Death are seen.

This is the River that " follows"
    Where'er we go :
No sand so dry and thirsty
    But these strange waters flow.

To fainting men in the desert
    No *living* streams appear ;
But the waters of Death rise softly,
    Solemn and clear.

And down to the silent River,
    By night and day,
Old men and maidens wander ever,
    And pass away.

Some go with the voice of thanksgiving
    And melody ;
And some in silence at midnight,
    When none are by.

Some go where the smiling meadows
    Sweep to the River-side,
And the pale, sweet flowers are blowing
    Close to the solemn tide.

They wander gently downward,
    As the sun sinks low,
And linger amongst the pleasant flowers
    In the purple glow—

Till they hear a strange wind blowing
    Across the tide,
And a long, low sigh through the rushes
    By the River-side,

And the hour is come for crossing
    To the silent shore :
We may watch and wait for their coming,--
    They shall return no more.

And some are summoned at midnight,
    To cross in haste
Where the banks are steep and frowning,
    And the land lies waste :

No tender smiling of sunset,
    No pale death-flowers,
Which can make the banks of the River sweet
    In dying hours ;

Only a sudden leaping
    From the frowning height
To the cold dark breast of the River—
    And then the silence of night.

Many waters go softly dreaming
    On to the sea ;
But the River of Death floweth softest
    To thee and me.

We have trod the sands of the desert
    Under a burning sun :
Oh, sweet will the touch of the waters be
    To feet whose journey is done !

6

Unto Him whose love has washed us
  Whiter than snow,
We shall pass through the shallow River
  With hearts a-glow.

For the Lord's voice on the waters
  Lingereth sweet :
" He that *is* washed needeth only
  To wash his feet."

NOT FORSAKEN.

"The Master saith, Where is the guest-chamber?"

THE day was ended, and the shadows fell
    Along the street. I heard a distant bell,
    That seemed to ring in heaven, so soft and
        faint
        Its voice upon the air. I thought, Some saint
Is summoned Home—some soul will recognize
The low mysterious call, and will arise
To go unto the Father. Ah! for me
Will any sweet home-going ever be?
I made my nest too dear on earth; and now
That God has swept it bare, will He allow
My hope to build in Heaven?
                   I stood beside
My door—the door that might be left so wide,
For there were none within to feel the chill
Of the evening wind; and men were passing still

Each to his home and friends; the street would
    soon
Be cold and wide beneath the pale Spring moon.
And as I listened to the hurried beat
Of those home-going footsteps, still more sweet
And more appealing came the heavenly call
Of that soft bell, which seemed to pray us all
To look Above, and see how faint and far
The lights were gleaming where God's mansions are
But I had suffered loss, and sought in vain
To comfort me, and to forget the pain
Of Desolation in my heart.   Can skies
That sweep above me, grand with mysteries,
And rich in worlds of light, atone to me
For one lost smile on earth?   Alas! that smile
To me was sun and stars.   A little while,
And it was darkened.

                Lord, I worship Thee
Alone to-night—alone, and desolate.
How sweet it was for two to watch the gate
Of Paradise!—how sad for one to stand
And look alone across a dreary land,
And think how long the journey to the grave!
To-night I see no golden banners wave
Along the towers of heaven; I hear no sound
Of victors shouting loud on Holy Ground;

And ever as I look along the street,
And watch the passers-by, and hear the sweet
Low calling of the bell, I am aware
Of the dead silence in the House, nor dare
To turn and look within.

             Better to stand
Here at the door, and watch the shining band
Of stars led forth by God, although their light
Can comfort me no more. Those glances
    bright,
In times gone by, did thrill me; all sweet things
In Heaven and Earth were full of murmurings—
Vague, infinite, and beautiful—as the sound
Of many waters. On enchanted Ground
Our feet were standing then : now silence falls
On me, who stand alone. The jasper walls
Gleamed on me awfully to-night, as set
The burning sun on earth ; and, stranger yet,
The gentle moon is turned to be my foe,
Reproaching me from heaven : I loved her so
In the dear time that's gone ; but all things now
Look sorrowful on me.

             One dwelt awhile
In the guest-chamber of my heart, whose smile
Made summer sunshine all the year to me ;
Whose lightest word broke, rich in melody,

To cheer my soul.   But Winter came ; my guest
Went forth, with sad face, toward a clouded West,
And I was left alone.
               That bitter night
I sat astonished, till the unmeaning light
Of dawn broke on my heart, and showed how bare
It was.   The evening and the morning were
The first day of an empty life to me.
I rose, and set my window wide to the free
Fresh East, and knelt as I was used.   May He
Who loved us unto death, forget the prayer
I prayed that day !
              The angels standing fair,
Hand clasped in hand, around the Throne of
    Love,
With deep untroubled hearts, that never strove
To bear the sense of loss, could never know
To pity me.   But Thou, the unspeakable glow
Of Godhead, brighter than the sun at noon,
Dwells on a Face which, pale beneath the moon,
Was kissed by a betrayer ; and those eyes
Bear in their infinite depths the memories
Of lonely tears and watchings.   It is said
They all—His dearest—left their Lord and fled.
I have not been betrayed, only bereft
Of my soul's Treasure ere the noon, and left

To live an empty life; yet pity me
From the dim heights of woe, which were to Thee
Mysteriously familiar. Thou wilt blot
From Thy dread Book the bitter prayer which sought
No pity then.

            I rose at length, and swept
My heart, and garnished it, and never wept
When all the precious things were laid away
Which might remind me of the summer day,
Now gone for ever. All the morning hours
The sun poured richly through the windows wide
Into the vacant rooms. I brought sweet flowers,
And decked the house. "Let fragrant things abide
Even in the Chamber still, from which the guest
Is gone for ever. Here let sunshine rest,
And the glad breezes enter, laughing low
And treading soft. Then I shall come and go
Without this heavy sense of loneliness
Oppressing me. These simple guests will bless
The haunted Chamber.

               Still, I felt a Dread.
I felt it as the Presence of the Dead
Is felt through all the house, and not alone
In the dim Chamber, veiled with white, where moan
And prayer are stilled at last. The golden grace
Of sunlight, pouring through the desolate place,

Could neither warm nor cheer.   The chill of Death
Pierced me like bitter wind, and still its breath
Swept from that empty room.

                 I rose once more,
And, with a trembling hand, I locked the door,
And cast the key away.   " Henceforth shall none
Find lodging in my heart; why should I keep
A desolate guest-chamber, where the sun
And flowers grow pale, and where my soul must weep
Her shattered joy and life ?"

   *   *   *   *   *   *

                At length the night
Was closing in; the young moon, pale and bright,
Showed a deserted street.   That distant bell
Seemed to draw nearer, till its strange beats fell,
Like knockings of some hand, upon the door
Within my heart.

            At length it died away,
As soft waves die upon a silver shore ;
And as it sank to silence, suddenly
One stood before my house and spake to me.
A stranger's voice ; I had not heard its sound
In other days, yet surely with a bound
My heart leapt up to claim it, as the tone
Of one Beloved.

          He stood in the street alone,

And all the Night did seem to feel the power
Of that strange Presence, and the dark'ning hour
Trembled, as if the very dawn were there,
And the stars brightened in their courses, where
God's Angels drive them, gloriously fair.
And I—I felt His Presence, as the night
Had felt it, with a vague and soft delight,
As if *my* Dawn were come to me.

       Once more
He made, in the tone which thrilled my heart
 before,
The same request : " I would abide with thee
This night ;—forbid Me not, but let Me see
The chamber for thy guests."

       Alas ! that word
Did waken me, as with a sudden sword,
And I made answer (though I *think* I knew
Who spake to me): " This dreary, mournful place
Which once was Home to me, and showed a face
Of welcome unto all who came, is now
No longer meet for guests : I can allow
None such to enter."   I denied Him rest
And my heart's shelter ; he who loved Him best
Said, long ago, " He came to His own, and they
Received Him not ;"—it was fulfilled that day
Once more in me.

He did not speak.   He turned
And looked upon me.   How that strange look burned
Its image on my soul—so sad, so sweet,
So awful!—there I sank down at His feet,
And thought that Death had struck me with Christ's look
And hoped it too : alas! how would He brook,
In days to come, the sight of one whose door
Had thus been closed to Him?
                                        But bending o'er
My sinful head, He murmured, soft and low,
"God will forgive thee.   Father, be it so ;
He knew not what he said."   It was the voice
Of the High Priest interceding.   Men rejoice
At sudden sounds of music, but to me
Was given that night to hear the melody
Of music's secret Fountain.   Sweet it rose
Beneath the answering stars, ev'n as it flows
Where burns the sevenfold Sun.   I could have lain
All night at those dear feet ; but once again
He bent to me, and took me by the hand,
And I was given strength to rise, and stand
Before the Lord.
                        " Master," I said, with tears
And tremblings in the night, " if bitter years
Should be appointed me, because my soul
Refused so sweet a Guest, yet let them roll

All heavily and slowly over me
As chariots of wrath, till utterly
They crush my heart; I shall not think the fate
Too hard for such a sin.   And at the Gate
Of Death and Sorrow I will look for Thee !"
But He made answer, low and tenderly,
In the voice that charmed my very soul from me :
" The bitterness of Death behind thee lies,
And not before.   Henceforth shall mysteries
Of heavenly Love be with thee from the Lands
Of Light.   The chamber built for me of old
Was given to another ; but, behold !
This night I come—I come, whose right it is."
A low wind swept the street ; from heights of bliss
The fair stars smiled on us.   Still lower bent
The Master over me : " Thy soul is spent
With a most needless doubt ; thou shalt not tear
The lost one's image from thy heart ; forbear
The thought that I would have it so : to th' End
I loved *Mine* own.   I am the faithful Friend,
And know no change.   Thy steadfast prayer shall rise
     rise
Morning and evening, for the name that lies
So near thy heart."
                    Thus, more than Conqueror,
He entered.   As His fragrant garments swept

The threshold of the house, the inner door
Flew open for my Lord.

          A voice, that wept
In that lone chamber of my heart, was stilled
For ever at His entrance.   Music filled
The house—and Light, and Peace.

       *   *   *   *   *   *

          Oh, haunted soul,
Down whose dim corridors for ever roll
The voices of the dead ; whose Holy Ground
Re-echoes, at the midnight hour, with sound
Of feet that long ago were laid to rest
Yet trouble thee for ever ! lo, a Guest
Is waiting at the Gate ; and unto Him
Thou shalt bemoan thy Dead, and He will take
Sweet words and comfort thee.   Thine eyes are dim,
But stretch thine hands to Him ; He will not break
The bruised reed.

          Or, are thy dearest still
With thee on Earth, do their sweet voices fill
The house with singing ?   Let the fairest room
Be for the Master's use, and from His shrine
Blessing and peace shall rest on thee and thine.

ONE BY ONE.

" I will come again, and receive you unto Myself."
" The Master is come, and calleth for thee."

OT sweeping up together,
   In whirlwind or in cloud,
   In the hush of the Summer weather,
     Or when storms are thundering loud ;
    But one by one they go,
In the sweetness none may know.

In secret love the Master
  To each one whispers low.
" I am at hand ; work faster :
  Behold, the Sunset-glow !"
And each one smileth sweet
Who hears the Master's feet.

Have we not caught that smiling
  On some beloved face,

As if a Heavenly sound were wiling
   The soul from our earthly place?
The distant sound, and sweet,
Of the Master's coming feet.

We may clasp the loved one faster,
   And plead for a little while;
But who can resist the Master?
   And we read by that brightening smile
That the tread we may not hear
Is drawing surely near.

Or in the hush of the Summer weather,
   In the golden afternoon,
As we watch by a friend's sick-bed together,
   And murmur, " Better soon ;"
—Sudden, the Master's feet
May be heard in the sunny street !

Till then no dream of dying
   Had flashed through the sick man's heart,
But a sudden smile on his face is lying,
   And the soul rises up to depart
At the sound of those gentle feet,
Which come up through the sunny street.

Or perchance he lieth sleeping,
   With weary hand and head,
And does not hear our weeping,
   Nor the sound of that solemn tread,
Telling the hour is come
For his returning Home :

Then we whisper low together,
   " Behold, the Master's feet !
He comes through the sunny weather,
   Up by the smiling street ;
We had no thought, or fear,
That the hour had come so near :"

Then, trying to still our weeping.
   With trembling lips we say,
" We must break on this silent sleeping
   We must prepare *His* way ;"
And we stoop to murmur low,
" Are you ready, dear, to go?

" The Master is come, and calleth
   For thee ; He is at the door ;
Awake ! for His shadow falleth
   Already across the floor ;

Are you ready, dear, to go
With Him who loveth so ?"

Then a sudden voice of gladness,
   —As our earthlier voices cease ;—
" After my years of sadness,
   He bringeth tidings of Peace ;
How beautiful are His feet,
   Which shine from the Golden Street !"

And gently enters the Master,
   Through the room His garments sweep,
And our trembling hearts beat faster,
   And our eyes forget to weep—
Though we can hear Him say,
" Thou shalt be THERE to-day."

As one whom his mother comforts,
   He lays the soul on His breast,
But He draweth the curtains closely
   As it enters into Rest ;
And none may see it go,
Away through the sunset-glow :

He hath hushed the worn frame sweetly,
   He hath soothed the Death-alarms.

Till it lieth asleep completely
　In the Everlasting Arms;
We know not the soul is gone,
Till the Lord is found alone.

*　　　*　　　*　　　*

Or when the storm-rain dasheth
　Across the wintry night,
And the wild, red lightning flasheth.
　Like Angels' swords of light ;
And we pray for sailors' souls,
As the sea in thunder rolls :

Behold, as we kneel down trembling,
　The thunder crasheth free,
The Door bursts open wildly,
　And startled, we rise to see
—Serene, and still, and fair,
The Master standing there !

He looketh upon us sweetly,
　With his well-known greeting, " Peace,"
And He fills our hearts completely,
　And the sounds of the tempest cease;
But we know the hour is come
For one of us to go Home.

On all the sweet smile falleth
　Of Him who loveth so,
But to *one* the sweet Voice calleth,
　"Arise, and let us go;
They wait to welcome thee,
This night at Home, with Me."

—Not sweeping up together,
　In whirlwind or in cloud,
In the hush of the Summer weather,
　Or when storms are thundering loud;
But one by one we go,
In the sweetness none may know.

Not pressing through the Portals
　Of the Celestial Town,
An Army of fresh Immortals,
　By the Lord of Battles won ;
But one by one we come,
To the Gate of the Heavenly Home :

That all the Powers of Heaven
　May shout aloud to God,
As each new robe of Life is given,
　Bought by the Master's blood;

And the Heavenly raptures dawn
On the Pilgrims, one by one:

That to each the Voice of the Father
    May thrill in welcome sweet,
And round each the Angels gather
    With songs, on the shining street,
As one by one we go,
To the Glory none may know.

AMONG THE TREES.

I.—THE GARDEN OF EDEN.

HEARKEN ! The Voice of the Lord
Among the trees, the goings of the King
Stir the fair branches, in the golden air
Of Sunset.   Silently the soft dew falls,
And softly, while it falls, the Lord comes down
Like dew, upon His sinless earth ; and, lo !
The whole earth is at peace.   The Peace of God,
Which passeth understanding, keeps the heart
Of sinless man, ev'n as it keeps in Heaven
The Angel-hearts which burn before the Throne
With love untold.   And peace is on the face
Of Nature, for no sin hath raised its hand
To mar her ministry, and vex her in the work
Of showing forth the Glory of her King :
Her golden sun sinks gently in the west,
Her sweet, soft winds are blowing from the south,

And bear no sound of mourning on their wings,
And sweep across no graves.   And, lo! her King
Comes down at evening-time to give her light:
    Hearken! The Voice of the Lord!
The bending trees are murmuring at His Feet;
And, here and there, a little bird sings still,
Not trembling at His presence; and the sound
Of the four mighty rivers, as they go
Compassing all the Garden by their strength,
Makes a deep music in the twilight hour.
Hearken! It is a strong, triumphant Voice
That mingles with those voices; One who reigns
And mourns not, whatsoever may betide,
Is sending out His Voice, a mighty Voice.
    Hearken! The Voice of the Lord!
And hearken yet again: the Voice of God
Hath sounded; and behold the voice of man
Makes answer gladly; a most reverent voice,
As well becometh his humanity,
His frail, created soul and body, made
By Him whose Voice hath sounded: yet a calm,
Untroubled steadfastness is in the tone
Of him who answers, and a boundless trust
In God's great love.   Thus, standing in his fair,
Unspotted garments, lifting up his face,
Which hath no stain, unto the face of God,

Man answered to the Voice.   And in the sweet,
Still sky the moon came forth to walk in white;
And God, the Blessed, with His blessed child
Held commune, and the Angels went and came.
And yet, it might be only the low wind
Among the moonlit trees ;—but was there not,
After the Voice of God, a sudden sound
A little while ago, as of great wings
Of Cherubim, who passed upon the wind?
And, with the sound, the likeness of a sword
Seemed to flash by.   A *sword* in this sweet place!
Nay, let us hearken to the commune held
Among the trees : how blessed is this place,
Where God is worshipped by a sinless soul
In perfect love !   There is no Temple here,
For, even as it is in Heaven, God
Himself is Temple.   Hearken to the praise:
        And hearken, the Voice of the Lord !

II.—THE GARDEN OF GETHSEMANE.

Hearken ! The Voice of the Lord
Among the trees, the weary Olive-trees
Which have been wrestlers with the bitter storms
Of many years.   Now do they bend their heads
Above Another Wrestler, whom the storms
Of God are bursting on.   The river moans

A little in the vale, the angry clouds
Hurry across the sky, and leave no door
Open in Heaven. And upon the ground
The Dew is falling heavily, strange Dew
Of blood ; and hearken,—'mid the falling Dew,—
    Hearken ! The Voice of the Lord !
A Voice of prayer, a broken, human Voice,
Crying in agony, broken by tears,
Appealing to His Name who saves the poor
And sorrowful. The Voice of One who takes
A cup into His hand, whereof no man
May drink, and live. He takes it with a hand
Which trembles greatly, for the cup is red,
And full to overflowing with the wrath
Of God Almighty. In that same dread hour
The Lord's right hand did valiantly, for those
Whom He had loved ; He took the cup, and drank
And gave God thanks. Many shall call Him Blest
And shall sit down with Him, to drink the cup
Of joy at the Great Feast, for this His woe,
And for the deeper Woe which followed fast.
    Hearken ! The Voice of the Lord !
Few heeded it on earth ; what time He cried
In agony, His earthly servants slept,
And when He looked to see if any did
Take pity on Him, none were found to heed.

But to the ear of God His cry went up,
And, through the wide Halls of the Father's House
It echoed strangely; till the Sons of God
Stood silent in their places.   And the Voice
Of God spake out, commanding one to go
With heavenly consolations, unto Him
Whose cry came up before the holy Throne.
      Hearken! The Voice of the Lord!
The Angel in his shining garments stands
In the dim Garden, and beside the Man
Whose face is marred with sorrow, on whose brow
The shades of Death are gathering, and whose eyes
Are dim with tears and watchings.   And, behold!
The Angel veils his face with his white wings,—
His face which is so bright from Heaven's own sun,
His eyes which shine with an undying light,—
Before this Countenance, which is so worn,
So dim with anguish, and before those eyes
Which are so near to Death.   Yea, doth he veil
His face more closely, in the Presence high
Of this unconquerable love, this power
To suffer all things, even unto Death ;
Then he had veiled it, standing in the glow
Of the great Sapphire Throne, and knowing not
The depths and heights of this strong love of God.
      Hearken! The Voice of the Lord!

III.—THE GARDEN OF THE SEPULCHRE.

Hearken ! The *Silence* of the Lord
Among the trees ! We stand to listen here,
Beside the Garden Gate, and the sweet wind
Is rustling in the branches; and the stream
Is stirring, where the lilies stand and shine
In shady places ; and the little birds,
Which tremble not in presence of the Dead,
Sing sweetly; but their Lord is lying dumb,
In midst of all His creatures, dumb and dead.

Hearken ! The Silence of the Lord !
The broken voice, which pled with many tears
In the deep shadows of Gethsemane,
Is hushed, is done with tears and tremblings now,
The seal of death is pressed upon the mouth
Which spake as never any man did speak.
Let us put off our shoes from off our feet,
And draw a little nearer, to behold
The place where they have laid Him. This is
    He,
God's Just and Holy One, in whom no guile
Was found. The Lilies of the Valley stand
Around *His* grave, and live,—and the sweet Rose
From Sharon bendeth over Him, who called
Himself "The Rose"—living, while He is dead.

Yea, all His flowers are standing in the sun,
Arrayed in beauty, while He lieth wrapped
In darkness.   Oh, how dreadful is this place !
    Hearken ! The Silence of the Lord !
This Silence speaketh with a thunder-voice.
HE sleepeth in His bloody, borrowed tomb,
In darkness and in silence, with the dead ;
—And, lo ! the City that hath slain the King
Sleeps sweetly in the sunlight.   Carelessly
She had arranged, " His blood shall be on me,
And on my children—let Him die the death :"
And now she resteth, vexed by Him no more,
And at her ease; and, lo ! she knoweth not
That He has left her desolate.   She sleeps
In quietness, and the sun is on her face,
And all her dreams are sunny.   Never heed
The blood upon her garments—never heed
Although there lieth, at the City Gate,
A Lamb as it had been slain.   Was it not meet
That one should die for all her people ? See !
She smileth in her sleep, and will sleep on
Till, in God's time, in the set time of Him
Whom she hath slain, she must wake up to hear
God's Judgments thunder at the City Gates
Demanding blood for Blood.   Then shall she be
Most desolate of cities.   *Now*, she sleeps ;

And hearken! The Silence of the Lord!
O piercèd hands, that were stretched out in vain
All day to man, and stretchèd out at last—
But not in vain—for man upon the Tree,
At rest at last. O weary, wounded head,
Marked with the Crown! He said He had no place
To lay His head, but He hath found a place.
O feet, that hath been weary with the hills
Of Ephraim and Judah,—going oft
By stony mountain-tracks to seek His sheep,
The lost sheep, scattered on the burning hills
Of Israel ;—at rest, at rest, at last!

    Hearken! The Silence of the Lord!
For God hath given His BELOVED sleep,
And, through the sunny, sacred Sabbath hours,
He takes His Sabbath rest, for all His work
Is done. And, lo! the Lord hath given charge
Concerning Him unto His Angels ; and,
Until the Day dawn, they do compass round
The Sleeper. No one shall break through, to stir
Our Love up till He please. Behold, how sweet
And fragrant is His rest! even these sad
Death-garments smell of myrrh and precious spice.
As it was written all His garments should,
For God hath given His Beloved sleep!

    Hearken! The Silence of the Lord!

IV. —THE GARDEN OF PARADISE.

Hearken ! The Voice of the Lord
Among the trees !   Forth by the waters still
Of everlasting comfort, He doth lead
His people ; and their sun shall set no more,
And no rough winds shall ever rise. to blow
Upon their heads.   For God Himself doth keep
This Garden : every moment with His dews
Doth water it, and shine upon it with
His Face.   What time the sweet south winds do blow
Upon the Garden, all the spices cast
Their fragrance forth, and all the trees are stirred
To heavenly music, and the people walk
In white : and, lo ! the Lamb is in their midst.

Hearken ! The Voice of the Lord
Among the trees ! no more our fading trees,
Which grew amongst our graves, and shiver oft
In our rough winters, but fair trees that stand
On either side His River, where the smile
Of God is sunlight : trees whereon no harps
Of mourners hang.   Not coming down at eve,
To walk a little while, and then depart,
But, in this Garden walketh evermore
The King of Peace.   See ! this is He who lay
In the earth garden dead, for the great love

Wherewith He loved the Church. Now doth He live
For evermore ; and, lo ! the Church doth live,
And walk with Him from henceforth in the skies.
    Hearken ! The Voice of the Lord !
And hearken yet again ; for when His Voice
Hath sounded out, behold, the voice of man
Makes answer gladly. These be His redeemed,
Who cease not, day nor night, to worship Him
Who once was slain. Hearken ! the thunders roll
Across the River ! Those who go from us
To them, can catch the music, as they pass
Through the dim waters, to the further side,
—" Glory to God !" " Worthy the Lamb !" they cry
    Hearken ! The Voice of the Lord !
This is the Bridegroom's Voice. And we who stand
Outside the door, and hear His Voice within,
Rejoice, because we hear the Bridegroom speak
In tones of joy. On earth He was a Man
Of bitter sorrows : all the waves of God
Went over Him. But He is comforted,
And we rejoice for Him. A little while,
A little while, and we shall stand without
No more, to hear His Voice ; but enter in
With joy unspeakable, to see His Face.

THE MEETING PLACE.

THE daylight has faded over the sea,
        The shadows are gathering heavily,
        The waters are moaning drearily,
        And there is no haven in sight for me,—
            Only a black, wild, angry haven ;
    Only a rolling, moaning sea ;
And a small, weak bark by the tempest driven
    Hither and thither helplessly.
For I am alone on this moaning sea ;
Alone, alone, on the wide, wild sea !
Only God stands by in the dark by me,
But his silence is worse to bear than the moan
    Of the dreary waters that will not stay ;
And I am alone—ay, *worse* than alone,
    For God stands by, and has nothing to say !
        And Death is creeping over to me,—

Creeping across the drear black sea,—
Creeping into the boat with me!
And he will sink the small, weak bark,
And I shall float out in the dreary dark
 Dead, dead, on the wide, wild sea;
  A dead face up to the cruel sky—
Dead eyes that had wearied sore for the light,—
  A dead hand floating helplessly,
Tired with hard rowing through all the night;
  This is what thou shalt see, O God!
From thy warm, bright home beyond the cloud;
 Thou denied'st me light, though it overflowed,
And there was not room for it all in heaven,—
 Thou denied'st one ray unto me, O God!
By the windy storm and tempest driven;
 Thou shalt look on my lost face, God, and see
What it was to die in the dark for me!
But I cannot reach Him with this wild cry,—
 I cannot reach Him with this poor hand;
 Peaceful He dwells in the peaceful land,
And the smile on his face is untouched by me—
  Only another Eternity lost,
  Only another poor soul gone down,
 Far out at sea while He smileth on!
The songs of Heaven are loud and sweet,
And thrill His heart with joy; it is meet

That He should not catch the far-off moan
Of another soul undone—undone!
  Here we part, O God!
 Thou to thy life and light,
To the home where thy dear ones gather to Thee
 I to my Death and Night,
A lost thing, with nothing to do with Thee;
Drifting drearily out to sea.
Thou hast stood by me through my long despair,
Thou hast shut from Thee my feeble prayer;
  Let us part. O God!

    II.

Through the darkness over the sea
A voice came calling—calling to me,—
A gentle voice through the angry night,
And I thought, "Some one else is out to-night,
 Out—out—on the wide, wild sea;
 Can it be any one seeking me?"
So I answered as well as I could from my place,
Though the wind and rain were beating my
  face;
 And through the darkness—over the sea—
 Still the voice came calling, calling to me;
Nearer and nearer it came to me,
And one came into the boat from the sea.

The wind fell low round my little bark
As a wounded hand touched mine in the dark,
And a weary head on my breast was laid ;
And a trembling voice, as of one whom pain
    Had done to death, in a whisper said,—
    " I had nowhere else to lay my head."

III.

And it was *thus* that He came to me :
I had spoken against Him bitterly,
As of one who sat smiling on in heaven,-
    Smiling and resting peacefully,—
While I was perishing tempest-driven ;
    But it was *thus* that He came to me,
Through the deep waters struggling on,
Wherein standing or foothold found He none ;
The wild wind beating about His face,
Fainting and sinking in that dark place ;
He had been weary and far from home,
Struggling forsaken, alone—alone !

So out in the night on the wide, wild sea,
    When the wind was beating drearily,
    And the waters were moaning wearily,
I met with Him who had died for me.

8

THE MAN OF GOD FROM JUDAH.*

'ALAS, my Brother!
All the Land is still,
Deep-folded in the solemn wings of night;
And on the soft and dreamy plains of
Heaven
God leadeth forth His armies, to the sound
Of some celestial harmony.   The wind
That blew at sunset from the open Gates
Of the golden City,—which at evening-time
Stands smiling in the west,—has died away
Upon the distant sea.
The whole Earth rests,
And is at peace; content at heart, it seems,
After the glory of her sunset dreams,
To taste the soft mysterious gloom of Night,
And lie entranced beneath its darkened skies,
In something like that sleep, wherewith the Lord

* 1 Kings xiii.

Gives His Beloved rest.   Yet even now
There falls a voice of sorrow on the Night,—
The sweet calm Night, not made for troubled cry
And restless moan,—and still it says, "Alas!
Alas, my Brother!"
                         And behold the form
Of one who kneels beside a sepulchre,
And bitterly bemoans his Dead.   The stars
Shine on his lifted face,—an old man's face,—
Swept by the winds of sorrow and remorse.
"Alas, my Brother!   By this lonely grave;
His grave, and mine; how often have I knelt
Through burning days and bitter nights, to mourn
And weep for him.   In the hard winter-time,
When snow is on the hill, and icy storms
Sweep down from Lebanon, I mourn for him.
And when the spring-time comes, the flowers return,
And voices of the singing-birds are heard
Through all the Land, once more I mourn for him
No voice can reach him, in the Spring of the year,
Whispering sweetly, "Lo, the winter-time
Is past and gone, rise up and come away!"
He dreameth on, as careless of the Spring
And all the musical soft stir of life,
As of the troubled winds that fight and moan
Above his head in winter.

                              Yet a while,
A little while, and I shall go to him
Who will not come to me.   He, rising not
To let me in, yet draws me to his side,
And I shall shortly yield, and sleep with him
It may be that, this very night, my God,
After so long a time, will think of me
And call me into Peace.   He reckons up
The number of my sins ; He knows this stain
Of guiltless blood, that burns upon the hem
Of a Prophet's garment ; yet, my God, I think
That I, even I shall be as white as snow
When I am dead.   I know, or think I know,
That my Redeemer liveth.
                              O my God !—
Most terrible, most terrible,—to Thee
My heart repeats this night its history,
And, through the darkness, looketh to Thy Face.
Thou knowest, only Thou, the old, old years
When, in the Spring of life, my heart was Thine,
And Thou wert mine.   Then would I pass long days
And solemn nights, afar from homes of men,
That I might be alone, alone with Thee,
And hear Thy voice, and see, perhaps, some gleam
Of angel-feet upon the Desert-ground,
Making it joyful, as with Summer-showers.

No simple human pleasures, dear to hearts
More free than mine, had any charm for me :
I only lived to hear the voice of God,
For He had visited my soul, and mine
It was to bear the Prophet's glorious doom.
Thou knowest, Lord, because Thou knowest all,
And yet Thou knowest not (having no part
In flesh or blood) the thrill and throb of soul
And body, when to mortal lips is laid
Thy coal of living fire : *—and when our eyes,—
Used only to the curtained gloom of Earth,—
Are lightened suddenly to meet the Sun.
Thou knowest, but for angels ministering,
The Prophet's heart would fail and break, between
The rapture and the pain.   Oh ! blessed eyes
That see, before their time, Thy mysteries,
And blessed ears that hear Thy glorious voice
Peal through the rending sky ; but blessed too
Are those who have not seen, who have not heard,
And yet believe.   They walk, in faith and hope,
Through the soft darkness of a Summer-night,
Lighted by gleamings of the silver stars,
And see no awful glories of the Sun
Till the Dawn breaks in Death.   But, having seen
The brightness of Thy Presence, having felt

* Isaiah vi. 6.

The winds of Heaven blow upon my brow,
And having tasted of Thy cup, my God,
How could *I* ever be content to wait,
As other servants, in Thy courts by night ?—
And therefore went I mourning many days,
When visions of Thy Glory ceased to haunt
My waiting soul.   Was it for sin of mine
Thou hadst withdrawn ? or was my mission o'er ?
Thou knowest, Lord : I only know I mourned
Too bitterly and wildly at the Doors
Which Thou hadst closed in Heaven, seeking not
To wait by night, in humble trust, on Thee,
But ever thirsting, burning, for the Word
Which Thou hadst taken from me.

When the Storm
Broke suddenly at midnight through my dreams,
Hast Thou not seen me rise and hurry forth,
Braving the terrors of the awful night,
In hope of catching but one word from Thee ?
Ah ! how I vainly waited for but one
Articulate utterance of the Thunder-voice
Which shook both Earth and Heaven.   And when
    Dawn
Broke full of tender promise, low I knelt—
Praying that on its fragrant breath might come
The still small voice of God ; but the sweet wind

Swept silently across my prayers, and bore
Perhaps to other ears the messages
Refused to mine.   It was a bitter fight,
And Thou wert strong and silent, and I grew
More reckless, drawing further from Thy hand
For all that fervid longing, once again
To hear Thy voice.   Thou knowest how I dwelt
Alone amongst Thine enemies, and saw
Strange altars rising up to other gods,
And would not speak for Thee, as any man
Who loved Thee might have done — not being
      allowed
To speak with wonders and with signs from Heaven.
And that dark day, which was to see the King
Stand forth, defying God, before the Land,
I tarried, heavy and displeased, for Thee
Within my house ; yet would not kneel to pray
For my lost Israel, and would not weep
For Thy great Name denied.
                              The hours wore on,
And they returned to me, who had beheld
That morning's wonders.   I, a man bereft
And God-forsaken, heard how God that day
Had spoken to the King, and done great things
In all the people's sight.   I heard, and knew
Mine office taken by another.   God.

Who saw me waiting, panting for His Word,
As for the water pants the thirsty hart,
Had called a man across the distant hills,
And giv'n to him *my* word, *my* message dread,
My courage to defy Death and the King,
And vindicate God's glorious Name from wrong
And to my heart I said, I will arise
To seek the man who took my place this day:
For I must look into his face, and hear
His voice repeat the message,—dying then,
And leaving him mine office.   Dark and cold,
And cruel too, my heart that day: I smiled
To think how terrible the legacy
Which I would leave to him who took my place ;—
An office which a man would scarcely hold
And live,—a gift of burning coal, to hands
Which must not tremble, holding it for God,—
A robe of costly white, on which one stain
Meant shame and death.

               I went to seek the man,
And found him sitting, weary, by the way,
With that deep weariness I knew so well
When I too bore the Burden of the Lord.
I did not spare the man who came to take
My holy office ; I betrayed that day
The faithful soul to death.   I brought him home,

By that vain tale, that God, the God of Truth,
Had changed the thing He spake.

                    I brought him home,
And gave him meat and drink, against the Word
Which God had spoken.   He was weak and
    faint,
And worn with fasting; and he sat with me
To eat and drink.   And whilst we sat at meat,
And converse held, I almost loved the man,
Though he should take my place.

                  In that same hour,
The Prophet's inspiration I had sought
So eagerly from God through weary nights
And thirsty days, rushed in upon my soul.
Ah! God is terrible!   He gives to man
The gift too wildly sought, and gives it so
That we had rather died beneath His sword.
Once more my soul dilated, at the sound
Of Doors that opened to the Future.   High
My heart beat at the breath of God, once more
Breathing on me from Heav'n.   I knew not yet
What manner of Vision this should be, but full
My soul swept on between its banks, to meet
That Thunder of the Sea :—till the meaning burst
Articulate and awful from my mouth,
Searing the lips that spake it.

Thus I cried,
By sudden inspiration, to the man,
Who sat at mine own table, " Thou shalt die,
Dishonoured, and in exile : none shall sleep
Beside thee, whom thou lovest, for this day
Thou hast forgotten God, and disobeyed
The mandate of His mouth." And it was *I*,
I, who had tempted him with lying words,
Whom God appointed to pronounce His doom.
The Prophet whom I had betrayed, gazed full
Into my face (as one who meets with Death,
In some strange solitude, may look on him)
With eyes that slowly darkened, as they gazed,
Till all their light was quenched. A thick cloud
    swept
Between God and his soul, and at noon-day
The sun went down.
            And when I ceased to speak,—
Like a strong man awaking from a dream,
He sighed, and moved,—then rose up in our midst,
And with no word to me or mine, set forth
Alone upon his way.

     *   *   *   *   *

            I heard them speak
Around me, when I wakened from my swoon,
What time the sun was stooping toward the sea,

Of one who had been slain that day, and calm
Slept by the way, a Lion watching him.
I knew it must be *he*, and I arose,
And gathered up my wasted strength, to seek
And find my Dead.   It was for me alone
He waited there ; far, far from those he loved,
For me he lay in Death ; and only I,
Throughout all Israel, had right to mourn
And bury him.

              At length I found my Dead.
The sun was sinking in a burning sea,
And all the waiting hills around were swept
By changing lights ot purple and of gold,
And on the rich bright air the fragrance rose
Of evening flowers.   And thus I came to him.
The wild rash Monarch of the forest stood
And gazed toward him spell-bound, with eyes that
    wore
A glare of terror,—and I was aware
Of Angels keeping watch about the Dead,
With wings of terrible white, that took no glow
From all that glorious sunset in the West.
I wore no armour, like to his, who lay
Uplifted in the solemn arms of Death
Too high for fear or wrong; yet I,—undone,
Defenceless, weak in anguish and remorse,—

I braved them all !   I faced the Messenger
Of Death, who waited, eager for his prey,
Until the Angel-guard should move or change ;
And those white Angels, with their lightning swords,
And eyes more terrible to sinful men
Than sword or spear, I braved them at their
    watch ;
And worst of all to face—I strung myself
To meet the look of him I had betrayed,
Awful in death, and dark with the wrath of God
Which had awakened on him.   I knelt down
And saw his face.   O God, my God, this night,
And every night, I bless thee for that look
He wore in sleep !   The look of one, to whom
After a hopeless night had risen a Sun,
Too wonderful and sweet for waking eyes.
He lay asleep, forgiven and asleep.
Ah ! the closed eyes were not too darkly veiled
For me to read the secret of their light,
And the locked lips betrayed it, in a look·
Which said the soul had smiled at its going forth.
With something like a tear upon his cheek,
And something like a child's surprise and joy
At unexpected sight of home and friends,
He lay asleep.   Dear in the sight of God
The death of all His saints.

Was it this look,
Which angels saw on the great Prophet's face,
When, for one stain upon the whitest robe
Of meekness ever worn by saint on Earth.
He lay in Death, alone, upon the Mount?
Rejected from his leadership, denied
An entrance into the Belovèd Land,—
Yet given a most sweet vision of that Rest,
Prepared for Israel; and drawn at the last
So close to the forgiving heart of God,
Men say he died of that Divine caress.*
O God, who art so terrible to those
Who fail and fall beneath Thy Burden, still
Thy mercy waiteth, and Thou givest a man
Such peace at the last, as only broken hearts
Can taste, or dream of.

     *   *   *   *   *

                        Safe from Angel's sword
Or Lion's deadly spring, by help of God,
I knelt to gaze on him, with thanksgiving;
Then raised him up, and bore him from the place.
We travelled slowly home, my Dead and I,
And as we went, what awful questionings
I held with him! The moon came forth and walked
In solemn brightness with us through the night,

* Referring to the Jewish tradition that Moses died at the kiss of God

And God was with us as we went; our God
Who had dealt wondrously with him who slept,
And would forgive me also : though *my* sins
Are countless as the sands.   With that sweet look
Of heavenly comfort on my Brother's face,
God gave me peace.

                     I long to sleep with him
And know the secrets of that speechless Rest.
It may be that, this very night, my God,
After so long a time, will think on me
And call me to Himself.   And yet my soul
Is almost like a weanèd child, and rests,
Content in Him, and cannot *ask* for Death."

      *   *   *   *   *

The stars grow pale ; a low wind from the East
Is springing, faint and chill.

                  Now, fair on Earth
The new Day breaketh,—but a sweeter Dawn
Has visited the Prophet's weary heart,
And in its light he sleepeth.   For behold !
The silver cord was broken in the Night,
And the loosened soul has found its rest in God.

PASSING SOULS.

DAY and night God standeth,
  Scanning each soul as it landeth
  Pale from the Passion of Death,
  Cold from the cold dark River,—
  As staggering, blind with Death,
With trembling steps, yet fleet,
Over the stones of darkness
They stumble up to His feet.

Oh, might they but fall down there,
And not have to face the glare
Of His awful smile or frown !—
For a little space just to fall down
With white face hid at His feet,
And gather a little strength,
And hope for a little sweet,
After the bitter River,
And then to look up at length
And grasp at God's Forever !

But this can never be,
For the people pass over fast,—
Even as a stream across the Stream,
Or as the visions across a dream ;
As a cloud of doves to their windows fly.
The clouds of souls unto God flit by,
Sweeping across the dreary River
Day and night to the dread Forever.

After the Nameless Woe,
The struggle in darkness alone,
With the Angel dim and strong,
With the Angel of the River,
Who showeth mercy never,
What strength have we left to stand
On the shores of the shadowy Land
And to meet the Face of God ?

Day and night God standeth,
Scanning each soul as it landeth,
Bearing the anguished gaze
Of many a darkening face,
As the living souls wax faint and dim
Beneath a righteous frown from Him,
Seeing the last hope fall and fade.

As the spirits fail before Him,
And the souls that He had made.

Watching with pitying, yearning eyes
The souls that refused His Paradise,
And have nowhere else to go this day.—
Till the fearful winds of Night arise,
Sweeping the shuddering souls away
To the Land where none can hope or pray ;
Whilst again and again the bitter cry
Of those driven souls in agony
Re-echoes along the misty shore,
Where the dead are gathering evermore.

O homeless souls ! wind-driven and tost,
Henceforth to find no resting-place,
But ever along the shores of the Lost
To be swept by the living storms of God,—
Ye had a fair and bright abode
On the other side of the misty River,
Where ye would fain have dwelt for ever :
And ye would not hear the voice of One
Who sweetly prayed beneath moon and sun,—
Let Me prepare a place for thee
Beyond the River, to dwell with Me.

Day and night God standeth,
Scanning each soul as it landeth,—
Watching the dim, sweet smile
That shines in that shadowy place
On many a Death-washed face ;—
Watching to see the victor-light
In His children's eyes as they struggle free
From the waves of their dread Death-agony.

Day and night *Christ* standeth,
Scanning each soul as it landeth ;—
Over the floods He bendeth
With a face which hath been dead,
With a mouth which once did cry
From these waves in agony,
" The waters go over My head !"

And when His children rise
To pass through the dreary River,
To the Shore they had not trod,
Unto the Face of God,—
Though their eyes grow blind with Death,
And they stumble in the Stream
As men in a deadly dream,
Christ stretcheth forth His hand,—

A gentle, piercèd hand,—
And draws them safe to Land.

Not as the others came,
But holding fast by a mighty Name,—
With trembling smiles of victory—
As those who vanquish while they die—
They pass through the misty River.
To the shore of the dim Forever.

After the Nameless Woe,
After the dreary strife
Of the failing life with Death,
How sweet it will be to meet the glow
Of His smile who watcheth beside the River,
And to feel that the smile shall shine for ever

THE WELL OF BETHLEHEM.

I.

THE King was faint with battle ; and he stood
With weary face and garments rolled in blood
An exile from the city of his God.
The heat and burden of the day were sore ;
And he must see, with hope deferred, once more
The sunshine fade from every hill and dale,
And twilight fold his land of Israel.
His captains stood around him ; but the king
Forgot the clangour and the glittering
Of sword and spear, and all the pomp of war:
Towards the sunset stood the low gray hill
   Of Bethlehem afar.
He saw a vision of the old sweet days
   When, as the custom is in Israel,
His mother went along the shady ways
   By moonlight to the well :

Even in the desert hot and desolate
He felt again the touch of that sweet breeze
He heard the murmur of the olive-trees
   That wave beside the gate.

Fair vision this for warrior of might,
Athirst and weary from the headlong fight !
Above him fiery heavens, and beneath
The bitter waters of the Sea of Death :
And, " Oh, that one would bring to me," he said,
   " Or e'er it be too late,
Of the water from the Well of Bethlehem,
   Which is beside the gate ! "

Three mighty men, full armèd for the fight,
Burst through the foemen with resistless might,
   And brought unto the king,
     What time the night fell late,
   Of the water from the Well of Bethlehem,
     Which is beside the gate.

The king once more beside his captains stood,
And to the mighty men he bent his head.
" My warriors do great things for me," he said ;
" But this cup I do hold for these men's blood :
I may not drink—I pour it out to God."

II.

The Earth was faint with battle ; and she lay
With weary face and garments rolled in blood.
An exile from the presence of her God,
Through all the heat and burden of the day.
The noise confused of her great captains, shouting
    Hoarsely against each other in the fight,
And the deep voice of all creation groaning,
    Gave her no rest by either day or night :
And all her pleasant seas were turnèd now
To seas of death, and could not cool her brow.
And as she lay, and fevered with the pain
Of her long anguish, in a dream she turned again
To that sweet home which God had laid upon her breast
In the far spring-time for her children's rest ;
And His own presence in the garden, and His Word,
Which, mingled with the breeze, her soft trees stirred,
    Had given her a fountain ever sweet,
    And ever springing round His blessèd feet,
Where Earth might drink, and smile, and praise her Lord
And in her dream she lifted up her voice,
And, " Oh, that one would bring to me," she said,
    " While I in anguish wait,
Of the water from the Well of Paradise.
    Which is beside the gate ! "

A mighty Man, full armèd for the fight,
Burst through the foemen with resistless might—
Not heeding that the angel of the gate
Did pierce Him sorely with his sword of light-
    And brought unto the Earth,
      What time the night fell late,
    Of the water from the Well of Paradise,
      Which is beside the gate.

Meekly, with covered face and bended head,
" He hath done matchless things for me," she said
" This water I do hold for this Man's blood ;
I take the cup and drink—and live to God."

BEYOND THE SHADOW.

Written for the comfort of a dear friend, who had been speaking of one " gone before," and saying, " Oh, how I think of her at nights, lying out in the cold churchyard when the snow is on the ground!"

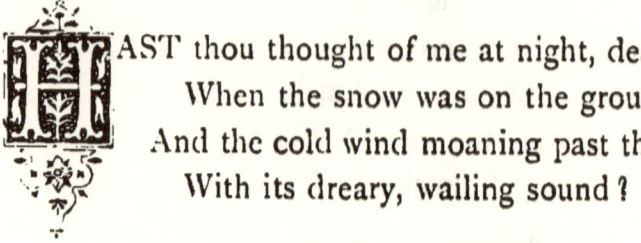AST thou thought of me at night, dear,
  When the snow was on the ground,
And the cold wind moaning past the house
  With its dreary, wailing sound?

When the rest were gathered gladly
  In the cheerful light at home,
And smiled and talked of their pleasant life,
  And of happy years to come—

While the storm beat on the window,
  And its voice was hoarse and loud—
Did thy thoughts go away from the smiling
    friends,
  To visit the friend in her shroud?—

To one who lay out in the storm there,
    Though the snow was on the hill,
And the rain beat wild on the graveyard,
    And her bed was low and chill ?

She, too, had sat in the fire-light,
    And smiled with life like these ;
Now let her lie still in her churchyard chill,
    With the snow about her face.

When they sang sweet songs to thee, dear–
    Those friends in their cheerful light—
Hast thou thought of the dreary voices
    That murmur across *my* night ?—

The voice of the night-wind wailing,
    The voice of the wild bird's cry,
The sound of the dead leaves falling,
    Where the dead men round me lie ?

Thou hast thought of me at nights, dear,
    When the snow was on the hill,
And the fire-light danced upon thy face,
    Though that snow on mine lay chill.

      *   *   *   *

I have thought of *thee* at night, dear,
　　Even as thou hast thought of me :
I—come to the quiet haven ;
　　Thou—out on the wintry sea.

I have thought of thee at night, dear,
　　When the night on earth went down :
And thou wert out in the cold, dear,
　　And I in the Father's home :

I—in the quiet City,
　　Where the sun shines evermore ;
Thou—out in the night, with thy fading light,
　　And thy face away from the door.

I have thought of thee at night, dear,
　　When the angels stood by me,
And the House was filled with the victor-song,
　　And the sound of the crystal sea :

For I knew that the songs of sorrow
　　Were the nearest unto thee,
And the sound of the dreary river
　　Which flows in the dark to the sea

We used to talk of the glory,
  When I, too, stood outside ;
Now I see the King in His beauty,
  In the far-off land abide.

But the half of all His glory
  Had never been told to me,
Nor the joy of the joyous city
  Which stands by the crystal sea.

I have spoken to Him at nights, dear,
  When I sat low down at His feet,
And the light of His overcoming smile
  Shone on till it seemed *too* sweet.

Too sweet for one so worthless :
  Yet I felt it set me free ;
And free to think of *thee*, dear—
  For He hath done all for *me*.

When the earth-wind sounded dreary
  Far away outside the gate,
I have said, " It bloweth chill on *her*
  Will she not be home till late ? "

The sun was on the City—
The sun on the golden street—
And the light of His smile shone on a while,
As His answer sounded sweet.

He spake in the speech of heaven,—
Which I may not tell to thee,
Save this, " I have rest and peace for *all*
Who seek for rest in Me."

So *He* thinks of thee at nights, dear,
When the cold night falls on thee,
And His voice goes down, through storm and sun
" There is rest, dear one, with Me."

And He'll think of thee at night, dear,
When the *last* night cometh down,
And the cold dew falleth, gleaming
In the last gleam of the sun.

When the death-wind from the valley
Moaneth through the forests dim,
"*We* will think of thee at night, dear,
And thou shalt think of *Him*."

GOD'S DOOR.

I.

"THE night is dark, the Door stands wide,
　　Oh, enter in and rest," they cried ;
　　" The night-wind moaneth down the street,
　　And the sound is over of passing feet,
　　And the city grows quiet and desolate,
—Thou art weary, the Door stands wide.
Oh, enter in and rest," they cried.

　　The night is dark, the Door is shut,
The cold wind moaneth down the street,
　　And one by one the lamps go out,
　　Along the road, as I stand without,
Without, in the cold, hard street.

　　The night is dark, I long to go
To my own bright home, in the home-like city ;

I have caught its gleam through the darkening hours,
As ever it gleams when the Tempest lowers,
To draw me back to its love and pity :
    But alone, afar, I must watch to-night,
    Till the Lord arise, and give me Light.
For I cannot go to my home in peace,
    I cannot rest at my own fireside,
    I cannot comfort my soul, and say,
    " We will come to the Door another day."
There is no more light, or comfort, or ease,
No home on earth evermore for me,
Except Christ let me in, and come forth with me.

I have caught the gleam of another Light,
    And the earthly joys have paled away.
I lay asleep in the empty night,
But God's touch wakened me up to see,
And the Light of the World shone on me.
A moment only, and then He was gone ;
    And a darkness grew up before my face
Which my other nights had never known :
    So I rose and passed through the darkening city,
Following Him who was gone before.
    I saw no Form, but some words of pity
Were murmured across the twilight hour,
And drew me along till I reached the Door.

But His voice is hushed, and the hours are long,
And the Door is shut, and barred, and strong,
And *He* is gone in, and has left me alone :
    Yet not alone, oh, not alone !
I see, by the light of the cold, wan moon,
That others are watching the Door with me ;
Old men and children, tremblingly,
Watching by God's shut Door, like me.

The watchers are pale in the dim moonlight,
And with tears they wait till the Master rise ;
And I think, as I see them stand in the night,
—A little while and those weary eyes
Shall see the Light.   But as for *me*,
It is harder to think that *I* shall see,
Though my heart is waiting too for Him.
    The sky is dark, the street is dim,
The night-wind moaneth coldly by,
And now and then I hear a sigh,
From those who watch the door with me ;
And now and then, when men go by,
I hear them laugh aloud, to see
How we wait in the night, O God, for Thee.

But the night wears on, the Door is shut,
And I tremble to stand so long without,

Lest I die before I enter in ;
For one came pressing up the street
A while ago, with hasty feet,
—One whom I did not care to greet,
One whom I did not dare to meet—
And I shook God's door with a sudden strain,
    When I heard the Sin-Avenger's feet ;
Yea, I shook the Door, in vain, in vain.

But I'll stand to the End at His fast-shut Gate ;
I will wait, and wait in the cold, hard street ;
    Perhaps in the dawn of the coming day,
    Perhaps when the night is on the wane,
He may hear the sound of my wandering feet
    About the Door, and may call me in.

II.

The night is dark, the Door is shut,
The cold wind moaneth down the street,
    And I, who stand no more without,
    Can hear the stormy Tempest's shout,
    And the call of the angry Sea.
He has brought me in, from the desolate street ;
He has brought me in, and my rest is sweet ;
    For the Lord doth comfort me.

The street was dark, the Door was shut,
The third watch of the night was come,
　　And all the dim lamps were gone out,
And we seemed no nearer God and Home ;
But the wind sank low in the dreary street,
And the sky grew softer, almost sweet,
And the stars came forth to gleam ;
　　The night was changed, and hope sprang up,
As hope might come in a dream.

I thought, I will try to trust in God ;
In the excellent Glory His abode
Hath been from of old ; thence looketh He,
And surely He cannot help seeing me.
And I think, perhaps He thinks of me ;
For my heart is with Him constantly,
And I cannot go from His door, and say
I have other good things, I will let Him stay.
So I'll try to think that He thinks of me,
And that His love holds me silently.

　　The night was dark, the Door was shut.
But sweet thoughts of the blessed Name
　　Of Him who died on Calvary
Swept through my heart; and then there came
10

Deep prayers that, in His mercy, He
Would cast His white robe over me :
I could not choose but kneel me down
—My face upon His Threshold-stone--
My heart embracing Him alone.

Then, as I prayed, I was aware
That some great Light was risen on me ;
And, looking upwards in my prayer,
I saw the Door was opened wide,
And One was standing at my side
It thrilled my heart to see.

And so He took me into rest,
From the dreary street with its shadows dim,
To the sweet, sweet rest His children know,
While their feet are tarrying still below.
The other rest remains with Him,
In the Upper Room of our Father's House,
Where the Feast is spread for the Master's friends,
And the song of their victory never ends.

The night is dark, the Door is shut,
I stand within the House of God ;
But I hear the wind, as it moans in the street,
And I hear the sound of the passing feet,

And sometimes I hear the trembling knock
Of one who standeth outside the Door,
Knocking and pleading more and more.

And I pray to Him who took *me* in,
To Him who forgave me all my sin,
That those who wait in the dreary street,
With trembling hands and weary feet,
May also enter into rest,
And dwell, like me, in His presence blest.

THE CHAMBER OF PEACE.

" The Pilgrim they laid in a large upper chamber, facing the sun-rising. The name of the chamber was Peace."—*Bunyan's Pilgrim's Progress.*

FTER the burden and heat of the day,
   The starry calm of night ;
After the rough and toilsome way,
   A sleep in the robe of white.

O blessèd Pilgrim ! we see thy face
   As an angel's face might seem,
For, lying pale in that shadowy place,
   Thou dreamest a golden dream.

The stars are watching the sleeping saint,
   And lighting the sleeping brow ;
But the light of the stars is cold and faint
   To the glory he dreameth now :

For the things that are hid from waking eyes
   Shine clear to the veilèd sight ;

From the chamber dim where the Pilgrim lies
   We can watch the fountains of light.

The journey is over, the fight is fought,
   He hath seen the Home of his love ;
And the smile on the dreamer's face is caught
   From the land of smiles above.

We also have sometimes lain asleep
   In the blessèd Chamber of Peace ;
Too weary to wrestle, or watch, or weep,
   For a while the struggle must cease—

We give thanks for the weakness that makes us lie
   So helpless and calm for a while ;
The roar of the battle goes hoarsely by,
   And we hear it, in dreams, with a smile.

Oh, sweet is the slumber wherewith the King
   Hath caused the weary to rest !
For, sleeping, we hear the angels sing,
   We lean on the Master's breast.

Thou hast another Chamber, dear Lord—
   The secret place of peace,
Where thy precious ones are safely stored,
   When their weary wanderings cease :

After the burden and heat of the day,
   The starry calm of night;
After the rough and toilsome way,
   A sleep in the robe of white.

The sacred Chamber is still and wide,
   You listen in vain for a breath;
And pale lie the sleepers, side by side,
   In the cold moonlight of death.

No sighs are heard in the shadowy place,
   No voices of them that weep;
They have fought the fight, and finished the
     race—
   God giveth them rest in sleep.

Are they dreaming, the sleepers pale and still ?
   For their faces are rapt and calm,
As though they were treading the Holy Hill,
   And hearkening the angels' psalm:

The things that were hid from waking eyes
   Shine clear to the veilèd sight:
In the last deep sleep the Pilgrims rise,
   To walk on the shores of Light.

Oh, sweet is the slumber wherewith the King
    Hath caused the weary to rest !
For, sleeping, they hear the angels sing,
    They lean on the Master's breast.

And sweet is the Chamber, silent and wide,
    Where lingers the holy smile
Of a wayfaring Man, who turned aside
    To rest, long ago, for a while :

He had suffered a sorrow which none may tell,
    He had purchased a Gift unpriced ;
When His work was over the moonlight fell
    On the sleeping face of Christ :

The face of a Victor, dead and crowned,
    With a smile divinely fair ;
The saints and martyrs sleeping around
    Were stirred as He entered there :*

His very Name is as ointment poured
    On the moonlight pale to-night ;
And the Chamber is sweet to Thy servants, Lord,
    For the scent of Thy raiment white.

---

* " And the graves were opened, and many bodies of the saints which slept
arose " (Matt. xxvii. 52).

The silent Chamber faceth the east,
    Faceth the dawn of the day,
And the shining feet of our great High Priest
    Shall break through the shadows gray.

The golden dawn of the Day of God
    Shall smite on the sealèd eyes ;
The trumpet's sound shall thunder around,
    The dreamers shall wake and rise.

The night is over, the sleep is slept,
    They are called from the shadowy place ;
The Pilgrims stand in the glorious land,
    And gaze on the Master's face.

NUMBERED WITH THE TRANSGRESSORS.

*" In a dream, in a vision of the night, when deep sleep falleth upon men, then
He openeth the ears of men, and sealeth their instruction."*

 LOOKED, and the soul of a child of God
Went up to God through the cloudy skies
At the hour of the evening sacrifice,
As the ransomed people go, one by one,
To inherit the Kingdom beyond the sun.
But not alone went the child of God,
By that unearthly, cloud-girt road,
For ONE bore him up as on eagles' wings.
They passed by the gates of the setting sun,
They passed by the pale stars one by one,
Which shone like the thrones of heavenly kings;
And the dark clouds swept through the darkening
sky,
Like chariots rushing before the Lord,
And the stormy northern winds flew by,
Fulfilling His royal and mighty word :

And, behold ! dark Angels, weary and tost,
(With the awful look of a Heaven lost
   On their faces grand and sad,)
Were passing athwart that stormy sky,
And shivered and moaned, as the Lord
     went by—
   Christ did not make *them* glad.

I looked till, up by the shadowy road,
They two were come to the City of God ;
And the glorious Angels, that ever stand
By the gate of the City, on either hand,
Beholding the royal face of Christ,
Cast down their crowns of gems unpriced
   Before those weary feet ;
And, "Lift up your heads on high, ye
     gates !
Behold, the King of Glory waits !"
   Rang down the golden street.

Methought, at that joyful Angel-shout,
On the face of Him who stood without,
Some thought, of infinite joy or woe,
Moved for a moment, mighty but dim :
I could not read which it was to Him,
And I did not see it come or go.

A moment He glanced up the shining street,
    Which no earthly sunbeams fill ;
A moment he looked where—awful, yet sweet—
    The Glory Inaccessible
Burneth upon the burning Throne,
In the midst of Heaven, uplifted, alone.
And again rose up the thunder-shout.
"Come in, Thou Blessed of God the Lord ;
Come in ; why standest *Thou* without ?
    We hail Thy coming feet ;"
And, " Lift up your heads on high, ye gates !
Behold, the King of Glory waits !"
Rang down the golden street.

And then it seemed to me there fell,
    As falls in a dream by night,
Perhaps an echo, perhaps a voice,
But those mighty Angels did so rejoice,
    I could not hear aright,
—" Father, if it be possible,—
Behold, *I* stand at the door this night ;
If it be possible :"—but from the Light
Of the Glory Inaccessible,
Which burneth ever, awful and still,
No voice made answer.   And then I think
He said, speaking softly, " Shall I not drink

The cup that My Father giveth Me ?
Surely I bear the heavy sin
Of many, and cannot enter in
To the Holy City of God the King.
Thou shalt go in, My ransomed one !
Behold, the doors stand wide for thee !
Behold, upon thy head the sun
Of God is shining !   As for Me,
I go to pay the Price, for thee
And many, who shall walk in white
Before the Throne of God this night.
A little while, and *My* feet shall stand
    Within thy gates, Jerusalem !
A little while, and from the Land
    Of trouble and darkness *I* shall come
    And sit down to My rest at Home."

There were *two* who went by the shadowy
    road,
And *two* who stood by the City of God ;
But up through the golden-shining street
One passed alone, and all the sweet
Mysterious joys laid up for those
Whom God has loved, infolded *one*
Of those two who went up by the setting
    sun.

The Other stood, in the deepening night,
Far, far beneath the starry Height
    Where the golden ramparts gleam ;
And in the night, the dreary night,
—" My God, Thy will is My delight ;
 —My People, ye *shall* win the Height ;"
    I heard Him say in my dream.

THROUGH THE FLOOD ON FOOT.

THE sun had sunk in the West
        For a little while,
    And the clouds which had gathered
        to see him die
    Had caught his dying smile.

We sat in the door of our Tent,
    In the cool of the day,
Towards the quiet meadow
    Where misty shadows lay,

And over the mountains of Moab
    Afar,
We saw the first, sweet gleam
    Of the first star.

The great and terrible Land
    Of Wilderness and drought.

Lay in the shadows behind us,
    For the Lord had brought us out.

The great and terrible River,
    Though shrouded still from view,
Lay in the shadows before us,
    But the Lord would bear us through.

In the stillness and the star-light,
    In sight of the Blessed Land,
We thought of the bygone Desert-life,
    And the burning, blinding sand.

Many a dreary sunset,
    Many a dreary dawn,
We had watched upon those desert hills
    As we pressed slowly on.

Yet sweet had been the silent dews
    Which from God's Presence fell,
And the still hours of resting
    By Palm-tree and by Well,

Till we pitched our Tent at last,
    The Desert done,

Where we saw the hills of the Holy Land
   Gleam in our sinking sun :

And we sat in the door of our Tent,
   In the cool of the day,
Towards the quiet meadow
   Where misty shadows lay :

We were talking about the King,
   And our elder Brother,
As we were used often to speak
   One to another,

—The Lord standing quietly by,
   In the shadows dim,
Smiling perhaps, in the dark, to hear
   Our sweet, sweet talk of Him.

" I think in a little while,"
   I said at length,
" We shall see His Face in the City
   Of everlasting strength,

" And sit down under the shadow
   Of His smile,

With great delight and thanksgiving,
    To rest a while."

 ·" But the River—the awful River,
    In the dying light,"
—And, even as he spoke, the murmur
    Of a River rose on the night !

And One came up through the meadow,
    Where the mists lay dim,
Till He stood by my friend in the star-light,
    And spake to him :—

" I have come to call thee Home,"
    Said our veilèd Guest ;
" The terrible journey of life is done,—
    I will take thee into Rest.

" Arise ! thou shalt come to the Palace,
    To rest thee for ever ;"
 —And He pointed across the dark meadow,
    And down to the River.

And my friend rose up in the shadows,
    And turned to me,—
      11

" Be of good cheer," I said faintly,
  " For He calleth thee."

For I knew, by His loving Voice,
  His kingly word,
The veilèd Guest in the star-light dim
  Was Christ, the Lord.

So we three went slowly down
  To the River-side,
Till we stood in the heavy shadows
  By the black, wild tide.

I could hear that the Lord was speaking
  Deep words of grace,
I could see their blessed reflection
  On my friend's pale face.

The strong and desolate tide
  Was hurrying wildly past,
As he turned to take my hand once more,
  And say Farewell, at last.

" Farewell—I cannot fear;
  Oh, seest *thou* His grace?"

And even as he spoke, he turned
  Again to the Master's Face.

So they two went closer down
  To the River-side,
And stood in the heavy shadows
  By the black, wild tide.

But when the feet of the Lord
  Were come to the waters dim,
They rose to stand, on either hand,
  And left a path for Him ;

So they two passed over swiftly
  Towards the Goal,
But the wistful, longing gaze
  Of the passing soul

Grew only more rapt and joyful
  As he clasped the Master's hand—
I think, or ever he was aware
  They were come to the Holy Land.

Now I sit alone in the door of my Tent
  In the cool of the day,

Towards the quiet meadow
    Where misty shadows play.

The great and terrible Land
    Of Wilderness and drought
Lies in the shadows behind me,
    For the Lord hath brought me out ;

The great and terrible River
    I stood that night to view,
Lies in the shadows before me—
    But the Lord will bear me through.

THE DYING THIEF.

PRISON, and the face of one who stands
To watch the dawning day.

The stars grow dim
In those pale skies above, and with a chill
And trembling sigh, the feeble morning wakes
He stands to watch the dawning of the day—
His own last day.   Fair on that sin-worn face
All night the moon hath shone, the paschal moon
Which walketh brightly.   And he could not sleep,
But paced the floor with restless, weary feet ;
And now and then the bitter words would break
Upon the tranquil moonlight :

"It is come
To this at last !   All things are lost to me !
And now they take my life.   O God ! to think
That I must die !—must die in my full strength,
With all this wealth of life, which beats and burns
Through every vein !   Oh, it is well for old

And worn-out men to die ! They sink and fail
By slow degrees, and lie at last so pale
Within the Shadow, none who watch them know
Whether they sleep or wake.   But for a man
To die in his full strength—so to be cast
Alive into the cruel arms of Death—
This is a bitter thing !   How dare they take
The precious years I might have lived from me,
And hurry me into a dreary grave,
And hide me from the light ?"
                                    But still the moon
Shone smiling in his face, and there was none
To pity him ; until in thought he passed
Forth of his prison-gates.   He trod once more
A well-known path, across the desert-hills
Of wild Judæa, and by moonlight saw
A far-off city, where the sad, sweet sound
Of Jordan's waves is heard.   The palm-trees there
Are waving in the night wind, and the moon
Kisses a quiet grave.   " Oh, well for him
Who sleeps this night so calm !   O father's face
Sealed to an endless peace ! no sin of mine,
No doom of mine, can trouble thee, to mar
The long night's rest !"
                                    But as he pauses there
In thought beside the grave, he seems to hear

A far-off weeping, as it were the voice
Of one who prays in agony. " Alas !
Alas ! for her who weeps this night beside
The Jordan's lonely wave ! No peaceful tomb
Has welcomed *her* to rest ; her very love
Has held her still awake from that last sleep,
To watch and pray for me ; as through the night
It held her eyes awake in bygone years
Whilst I was wandering far.   O mother's heart,
That will not rest !   All vainly dost thou wake
And weep for me.   I hasten to my doom,
Cast off by God and man."

           The far-off grave
Has faded from his sight ; the far-off sound
Of weeping dies away.   No palm-tree shade
Is o'er him now ; he hears no more sweet tread
Of moon-lit waters.   Dreary prison-walls
Are round him once again, and death is near.
Waiting in silence.   And, behold, the dawn !
The morning lieth faint and pale, outspread
Upon the mountains gray.

           He speaks once more :
" Life has been cruel to me ; Death is kind,
And Death shall comfort me !   I long to lie
In some dim place, and rest ; ere night shall fall
Like dew upon the hills which compass round

The Holy City, I shall lie and sleep
A dreamless sleep.   None shall have care of me
But only Death himself, and he will seal
The stone above me, hiding me from scorn,
And cruelty, and shame ; and I shall be
As precious in his sight as other men,
And I shall sleep as sweetly as the priests
From God's own Temple sleep around the hill
Where they have served Him.   Death receives us all
With equal love ; and, lo ! the iron gates
Stand open day and night ; the poor and sad,
Whom no man seeketh after, all are free
To enter there and sleep.   I go to Death,
And Death shall give me rest."

                "Come unto Me,
And I will give you rest !"

                  " Once more the voice
Is in mine ear.   It seems to echo now
The mournful hope that Death should give me rest ;
And yet I know this is no dream-like sound
Of sad Death making answer.   This the voice
Of Life, and not of Death ; it steals to me
With that faint sighing from the crystal east,
That sweet breath of the day.   I know not how
The words have power to haunt me.   Long ago
I heard them from a Stranger,—one who turned

And looked upon me as I passed, and seemed
To know my face, although I knew Him not.
Upon a green hill-side He stood ; the wind
Was rough that day, and pushed His hair aside ;
And, lo ! the face was weary.   Yet He spake
Of giving rest !   *He* needed rest, I think.
But patiently He stood, and spoke to those
Who gathered round Him ; and He turned His face
And looked upon me, as I passed them by
With careless haste.   He could not know how wild
And sinful was my life—a robber's life
Among the rocks and caves ; and yet He looked
As though He knew it all, and, knowing, longed
To save me from it.   No such yearning look
Had ever followed me, save from those eyes
Which are grown dim with weeping, far away,
Before the Lord for me,—my mother's look
Of love, which many waters cannot drown,
Nor floods of tears, which I have made her weep,
Can ever wash away.   The Stranger's look
Did mind me of her ; and He stretched His hand
'Come unto Me, to Me,' He said, 'and I
Will give you rest !'
                              I had no time to wait,
And went my way in haste, not turning back
To see His face again.   And yet I know

That sad look followed me.   It almost seemed
As if He thought that we should meet again
In some strange scene ; for many things had place
In that deep look of His.   It could not be
The *past* that moved Him ; I had never seen
His face before.   Was it some future day,
When He and I should meet ?

                  I went again
To my rough dwelling in the robbers' cave,
And lived my reckless life.   Yet for awhile
My soul was haunted ; morn and eve the look
Returned on me.

            What had the Man to do
With silences of everlasting hills
In noonday heat, or stately march of stars
Across the midnight skies ?   Yet all things seemed
To testify of Him.   On rushing winds
Which swept the wilderness, He seemed to ride
And meet my soul.   And many times at night,
And in the golden dawn, He seemed to pass
Before the cave, and summon me once more
To follow Him.   I knew that this was all
A strange wild fancy: in a little while
I heard the voice no more ; it died away
Upon the moaning wind, it sank to sleep
Upon the desert-hill ; and I was left

Alone once more, alone with men as wild
And lost as I.   But still at times I thought
That surely I should meet the Stranger yet :
He had a kingly face, and looked as none
Whom He should summon to His side could choose
But do His bidding some day.
                       Thus I thought
When I was worn with sin, and then I hoped
That in the future I should meet with Him
And see His face again.   But all my thoughts
Were vain and idle, never more the voice
Entreated me, I never saw again
That look which followed me ; and now at length
The end is come ; there is no future now ;
And though on this last night the well-known
    voice
Has sweetly wakened once again, and called,
' Come unto Me, and I will give you rest,'
Oh, what is that to an imprisoned man
Who cannot go, by this pale dawn, to seek
For Him who calleth me ?   My soul grows faint ;
Oh, were there but a man to plead for me
Before my Judge, or tell me how my sin
Might yet be pardoned !   Lo ! the Passover
Was slain last night in Israël, but I—
A man cast out—have had no part nor lot

In holy things, no priest to plead for me.
No sacrifice for sin."

     " COME UNTO ME,
TO ME, THIS DAY, AND I WILL GIVE YOU REST!"

  *   *   *   *   *

A cross,—and one who hangs thereon, in sight
Of heaven and earth.

      The cruel nails are fast
In trembling hands and feet, the face is white
And changed with agony, the failing head
Is drooping heavily ; but still again,
And yet again, the weary eyes are raised
To seek the face of One who hangeth pale
Upon another cross : he hears no shrill
And taunting voices of the crowd beneath,
He marks no cruel looks of all that gaze
Upon the woful sight. He sees alone
That Face upon the cross. Oh, long, long look,
That searcheth there the deep and awful things
Which are of God.

      In his first agony
And horror he had joined with them that spake
Against the Lord, the Lamb, who gave Himself
That day for us. But when he met the look
Of those calm eyes,—he paused that instant ;
  pale

And trembling, stricken to the heart, and faint
At sight of Him.
          Again, and yet again,
The long. long look is fixed upon that Face
With deepening awe.   Here, in the valley dim
Of death and sighing, he has come to Him
Who called him long ago.   That windy day
Upon the free hill-side he knew Him not,
But now he searcheth in that dying Face
The precious things of God.   For this is Christ,
The long Desired of Israël.
               At length
The pale, glad lips have breathed the trembling prayer,
" O Lord, remember me !" The hosts of God,
With wistful angel-faces, bending low
Above their dying King, were surely stirred
To wonder at the cry.   Not one of all
The shining host had dared to speak to Him
In that dread hour of woe, when Heaven and Earth
Stood trembling and amazed ; yet, lo ! the voice
Of one who speaks to Him, who dares to pray,
" O Lord, remember me !" A sinful man
May make his pitiful appeal to Christ,
The sinner's Friend, where angels dare not speak :—
And sweetly from the dying lips that day
The answer came.

Oh, strange and solemn joy
Which broke upon the fading face of him
Who there received the promise : "Thou shalt be
In Paradise this night, this night, with Me."
And thus the Lord fulfilled His word.   He spake
Of giving rest, and on the bitter Cross
He gave the promised rest.   O Christ, the King !
We also wander on the desert hills,
Though haunted by Thy call, returning sweet
At morn and eve : we will not come to Thee
Till Thou hast nailed us to some bitter cross,
And *made* us look on Thine : and driven at last
To call on Thee with trembling and with tears,—
Thou lookest down in love, upbraiding not,
And promising the kingdom !
                         Thus it was
That day on Calvary.   Oh, solemn joy
Upon the faint and fading face of Him
Who died a Victor there, so strong to save ;—
And on the pardoned face, what mourning love,
What awe and thankfulness !   "Thus am I come
To Him at last.   The call is answered now
Which followed me so long.   I look this day
On Him whom I have pierced, and mourn for
      Him '
With bitter mourning.   Christ, my Passover,

Is sacrificed for me, my countless sins
Are heavy on His head; I mourn for Him
Whom I have pierced. Behold, He loveth me,
And gives Himself for me !

                  In days to come
His name shall be above all names on Earth
Or names in Heaven. And He shall stand at last
Upon Mount Zion, with the shining host
For whom He dies to-day. Thus must I look
Upon the joy before Him,—else His woe
Would slay my soul this day.

                    The peace of God
Which passeth understanding stealeth o'er
My failing heart. For I am come to Him,
To Him at last, and He has given me rest,
According to His word. Yea, hanging here
In sight of Heaven and Earth, a man cast out
And dying this slow death of pain and shame,
I rest. I rest in Him."

     *   *   *   *   *

                A Throne,—and one
Who kneels before it, bending low in new
And speechless joy.

                It is the night on Earth,
The shadows fall like dew upon the hills
Around the Holy City. But above,

Beyond the dark vale of the sky, beyond
The smiling of the stars, they meet once more
In peace and glory.   Heaven is comforted,—
For that strange warfare is accomplished now,
Her King returned with joy : and one who watched
The far-off morning in a prison dim,
And hung at noonday on the bitter cross,
Is kneeling at His feet, and tasteth now
The sweet, sweet opening of an endless joy.

I.

I HAVE heard the awful song
    Which the Sea is ever singing;
The tender, merciless song,
    Which to all the lands is ringing:
    " Come unto me,"
Saith the awful Sea,
  " And I will give you rest.
It is better to die than to live,
It is sweeter to sleep than to grieve;
  So come and sleep on my breast."
The faces under the Earth and Sea
Seem more patient, and joyful too, to me,
Than those that dwell on the smiling Earth
  And sail on the smiling Sea.
" Come unto me,"
Saith the awful Sea,
  " And I will give you rest.

12

A little struggle at first, of course,
A little gasping for one more breath,
A little agony,—nothing worse,—
　　And then the long sweet sleep of Death !"

II.

This is the awful song
　　Which the Sea is ever singing ;
The tender, merciless song,
　　Which to all the lands is ringing.
Oh ! the Ocean murdereth tenderly,
　　With soft blue waves which a child might
　　　　love :—
Only they creep so *very* near,
　　And close *so* strong above ;—
Gently forcing the struggles by,
　　Gently stealing away the breath,
Gently closing the mouth and eye,
　　Till the struggling face grows white in death.
And then when the strong and terrible Sea
　　Hath wrought its awful will,
It catcheth the poor form to its breast
　　And husheth it very still ;
In the winding waters' waving flow,
Swaying it softly to and fro
As the smiles of the great Sea come and go,

With a hushing, tender, motherly motion,
The awful, tender, merciless Ocean,
  And singing the old, old song,
  Which the Sea hath chanted long :
" It is better to die than to live,
It is sweeter to sleep than to grieve,---
  So Death is the kiss I give."

III.

And thus when we sail on the sounding Sea
  Far out of sight of land,
And on the gray watch-towers in the sky
  The stars come out to stand,
In the quiet, waving motion we feel
That the dead people lying far under the keel
  Are swaying softly to and fro
  As the smiles of the great Sea come and go
Very quiet and glad they must be,
Cradled so deep in the gentle Sea ;
For no man ever goes down in wrath,
By the wandering, waving, shifting path,
  To trouble them in their home ;
Only sometimes a quiet drowned guest
Comes slowly down to share their rest :
  For in answer to the song
  Which the Sea has chanted long,

Sailors and women silently come
　　Through the winding waters now and then,
　　And the great Sea murmurs—" Amen ! Amen
　　In the pauses of its song.

IV.

The faces under the Earth and Sea
Are more patient and joyful too than we,
For the grace of Christ on many a face
Maketh a light in the dim death-place ;
And swaying softly to and fro
As the smiles of the great Sea come and go,
Lies a fairer smile on the white, locked face
　　As if it, in some matchless mystery,
Were 'ware of the spirit standing high
Above all waves, in the starry sky,
　　On the silent crystal Sea.

PARTINGS.

I.

OWN in the Valley of Death,
  Where the shadows are strange and drear,
The midnight air is heavy with sighs,
  As of those that part in fear.
  And terrible visions pass,
Like winds across the night,
Of severed hearts, and hands unclasped
  That *had* been clasped so tight.
One goeth forth alone,
  An unknown Fate to face ;
And one, his friend and treasure lost,
  Goes back to his desolate place.

II.

Yet down in the Valley of Death
  A Cross is standing plain,

Where strange and awful the shadows sleep,
  And the ground has a deep red stain.
This Cross, uplifted here,
  Forbids, with voice Divine,
Our anguished hearts to break for the
    Dead
  Who have died and made no sign :
As they turned at length from us,
  Dear eyes that were heavy and dim
May have met His look who was lifted
    there—
  May be sleeping safe in Him.

III.

But down in the Valley of Death
  Are whispers low and sweet,
As the Pilgrim of Christ is marching through,
  And the Night and Morning meet ;
Whispers of faith and hope,
  Of a love that will not die,
And the dawning upon a weary heart
  Of the Dayspring from on high.
And one goes forth with joy
  To meet the Bridegroom's Face ;
And one gives thanks, and turns again
  To his work for a little space.

IV.

Down in the Valley of Death
  Lies the *Home* of parting pain :
Yet not alone in its solemn shade
  Are claspings wild and vain ;
On the broad rich plains of Life.
  Where the bright winds come and go,
Sweeping the golden fields of corn
  With a murmur soft and low,
A voice of parting tears
  May break on the morning's breath ;--
Is it harder to part in the glowing sun,
  Or down in the Valley of Death ?

V.

Our blessed Dead are wrapt
  And hidden from us by Love,
Till soul be knit to soul once more
  In the shining courts above.
Their burning hearts might shrink
  From hearts so cold as ours ;
Beneath their eyes, which cannot weep,
  Our tears might fall in showers ;
Their radiant brows would shame
  These care-worn brows of clay :

Ah ! it is well that we meet no more
   Till we are even as they !

VI.

But the living and the lost—
   For *them* our souls must weep ;
For them we suffer a yearning pain
   That will not let us sleep :
And ever we moan and say,
   Whilst the stars are calm and clear
Oh, for one look, one clasp of the hand,
   One tone of the voice so dear !
Oh, brilliant seas of Earth,
   That roll so bright between
Long-severed friends, ye show more dark
   Than Rivers of Death had been !

VII.

God takes them from our hands
   (That seemed but made to cling) ;
He sets them far away, in the shades
   Of His far-stretching wing,
And bids us pray for them
   With a deep and yearning thrill—
With a passionate power we had not known
   When they were with us still.

" He doeth all things well ! "
We say it now with tears ;
But we shall sing it with those we love
Through bright eternal years.

THE KING ETERNAL.

" A thousand years as one day."
" Not yet fifty years old."

I.

GLORY on glory compassed Him around
    From everlasting on to everlasting years ;
  And through the depths of glory rang the
      sound,
  The voices of the seraphs standing crowned,
  And glorifying God through all the years :
A thousand years of glory swept along
      Year after year ;
But on His face who sitteth on the throne
      No hope or fear
In all these wide long years had marked a change,
And unto Him came nothing sad or strange.

II.

The years told on Him heavily,
  And He was grown old before His time :

And it seemed so long since the sweet low chime
Of the angel-voices had died away
As He passed out from the Golden City,
   Through the starry spaces that round it lay,
And down, in the strength of His own strong pity,
   To our dark Earth rolling drearily ;
   And the years told on Him wearily.

III.

Glory on glory compasseth Him round,
From henceforth unto all the deathless years ;
The smile of God, wherewith He sitteth crowned,
   More sweet, because the memory of tears
   Is in His heart, and dieth not away :
And in exchange for every weary day
   He spent on Earth, some blessed soul forgiven--
Some face once darkened with our sin and night
Is lifted up to Him in cloudless light,
   And addeth glory to these days of Heaven.

OUR SAILOR LAD

PART I

ON the golden sands by the sea,
    As the sun drew near his rest,
We stood to watch the stately ship
    Ride slowly down to the West :
There sailed our gentle lad,
    With his face to the sunset lands ;
And our prayers went solemnly up to God
    As we stood with tears on the sands.

For the words which the lad had said
    At the farewell-hour that day,
Stole back on the golden air to us :
    " You must watch with me and pray ;
And I shall be safe on the sea
    When the waves and thunders roar,
For Christ is to sail in the ship with me
    And bear me safe to shore."

We watched : and the ship passed on,
   Like a spirit walking in white,
Along the shining path which the sun
   Had traced on the waters bright ;
And we saw till she seemed to sail
   Right into the glorious West,
As when a conqueror calmly rides
   At evening-time to his rest.

It seemed that the gates of God
   Were standing open wide ;
And the ship passed in on the floods of light,
   As upon a heavenly tide.
Had she swept through the Mystic Gates,
   And out on the Crystal Sea ?
Were the mariners gone through the shining West
   To the Haven where we would be ?

Ah ! many of us would launch
   With songs on the sunset tide !
But we but sail out on that quiet Sea,
   To land on the Heavenly side.
To be sailing away from sorrow,
   Sailing away from sin—
How sweet would be the voyage forth !
   How sweet the entering in !

There be many look forth at sunset
    From those golden gates of the West ;
We may sometimes catch their smile on the
        sea,
    And we fain would share their rest :
But not on a shining pathway
    Which the sun has traced on the sea,
And not in an earth-built ship we sail
    To the Land where we would be.

The vessel was wrapt away
    In the glorious folds of the West ;
Our sailor lad was in *His* care
    Who gives His loved ones rest.
The light of that vanished smile
    Ne'er shone so sweet before,
As it shone that night in our darkened home
    A memory—nothing more.

PART II.

By the moaning midnight sea,
    Whereon no pale star smiled—
By the black and storm-rent sea,
    When the winds were hoarse and wild—
We stood and cried to God
    For the ship that was nearing fast :

For we knew she was hurrying on to Death,
On that rough, resistless blast.

On the terrible water-floods
   He sitteth King and God ;
And upon the wings of angry winds
   His angels walk abroad.
The winds and thunders meet—
   The sea is rent beneath ;
We tremble lest their voices wild
   But cover the cry of Death !

" Once more to his father's house,
   To the land where he would be,
Lord, bring our gentle lad to-night
   Across the raging sea ! "
The winds were hurrying past,
   And caught the prayers away
From the trembling lips that uttered them,
   As from the waves the spray.

Yet we called on the mighty Name
   That never is named in vain :
The prayers were not lost, though swept away
   By the night-wind and the rain.

And the Lord God answered us
  Away on the stormy sea ;
For in that same hour the lad was gone
  To the LAND where he would be.

We had seen no opened Gate
  In the clouded Heavens that night—
Across the raging waves nad shone
  No path to the Land of Light :
Yet our sailor lad had found
  A way to the Throne of God ;
He was gone by the path which the thunder
    knows—
  The path which the tempests trod.

Not sailing softly forth
  On a golden sea to the West,
Where the way seems clear to the Heavenly side
  And the waves are hushed to rest ;
But forth, when the storms were out
  On a wild and dreary sea,
All through the starless dark he rode
  To the Land where he would be.

We had asked for an earthly thing
  That night, in the hour of dread ;

But the Lord had answered all our prayers
  With a heavenly thing instead—
Receiving our sailor lad
  To the Haven calm and blest,
To a sunnier Home than we could give,
  And a more enduring Rest.

A heavenly thing for *us*,
  As well as for him we love,
To have one so dear in glory set
  At the King's right hand above.
Yet our hearts had wearied sore
  To see him face to face :
It is sometimes hard to rejoice that he
  Attained to the holier Place.

Yet still we bless the Lord,
  And still we wait to see
Our sailor lad in a little while
  In the Land where we would be ;
For on calm and golden seas,
  Or tossed by wave and blast,
Each soul which Christ hath bought must come
  To the Heavenly Shore at last.

13

TROUBLE NOT THE MASTER.

" ROUBLE Him not in the dawning
    Of His brief and bitter day,
    Dreamlike spreadeth the morning
       On the mountains chill and gray :
    Let Him rest for a little while,
  Let the stars of the morning smile
    On the head so soon to bear
    The noonday's burning glare.

" The dews of the Dawn are falling,
    And the Earth her moaning stills ;
  She has heard the Angels calling
    Once more on her starlit hills :
  And more than the Eden-sweetness
    Comes over her heart to-night,
  At the tread of the Angel-Watchmen,
    And the touch of the raiment white ;

For she knows that once more they hold her dear,
And from this night forth, with joy and fear,
Will often come down from the golden Gate
    Of the Glory undefiled,
And be glad in the dark of the Earth to wait
    And watch by a little Child.

" At midnight her mountains trembled
    As with the tread of God,
And all the Heavens were shaken
    By winds from cloud to cloud ;—
But hushed was stormy sighing
    Of winds and clouds to rest,
As God stooped low from His holy Hill
    And laid the Child on her breast ;
Let Him rest for a little while,
Let the stars of the morning smile
    Over His head, with tremblings sweet—
They used to tremble beneath His feet !

" Trouble Him not in the dawning
    Of His brief and bitter day :
He is not used to mourning,
    Nor to weary faces of clay ;
And ye have no voices of angels
    Wherewith to sing to Him ;

No crowns to cast before His feet,
No smiles, with glory dim and sweet,
  Like His crownèd Seraphim :
In the dimness and gray of the dawning
  They are standing with wings outspread.
With lightning wings, that used to glow
In the smile of Him who lieth low
  This night on His earthly bed :
Let Him rest for a little while,
Let the Morning-Angels smile,
  And sing in the twilight dim
  Some heavenly song to Him.

" Yet,—come to Him in the dawning
  Of His brief and bitter day :
For unto *you* the Child is born,
And for you He lies forlorn
  In the shadows chill and gray ;
And to you are His angels calling
  Among the star-lit hills,
Where the dews of the dawn are falling
  On the flowers by the misty rills,—
Holding on high the Eastern Star
To guide you from the plains afar :
For, not unto them, but to us is given
  This night the Holy Child ;

And ye must go and kneel to Him,
Though your hearts with sin be changed and
    dim,
And though He is undefiled ;—

" Though your faces sad and weary,
    And your eyes so worn with tears,
Must foreshadow to Him the human woes
    He shall bear through the dark'ning years—
Must remind Him of the awful price
    To be paid for such as we,
In the hour when His sun goes down at noon,
And God shall send nor star nor moon
    To shine upon Calvary."

So the shepherds have left their watching,
    And risen to meet the King,
Who is come from the Throne of God on
    high
The tidings of Peace to bring :
In the dimness and gray of the dawning,
    Behold, they are bending low ;
And the sages are hast'ning from eastern hills
    Where the mystic Star doth glow:
And we count them blessed servants
    Whom their Lord, when He came to-night,

Found ready to trust the joyful news,
  And to hail Him Life and Light ;
Let them kneel for a little while,
Let the stars of the morning smile
    On the faces of those for whom the King
    Shall make of His soul an offering.

II.

Trouble Him not in the dawning
  Of His bright eternal Day ;
Glorious riseth the morning
  On the Face where the shadows lay.
He standeth afar on the mountains
  Of frankincense and myrrh,
Where the winds of Heaven sweetly blow
  And the golden rivers stir.
Let Him stand on His holy Hill,
And let Heaven and Earth be still
    Before the face of the Conqueror,
    Whose arm was glorious in the war.

Trouble Him not in the dawning
  Of His fair and endless Day ;
Let no hoarse voice of mourning
  Go up from the shadows gray :

Let Him stand on the Heavens, uplifted
   Beyond the sound of woe,
And only the angels speak to Him
With wondering faces, waxing dim
   And bending ever low—
As the glory of His lifted face
Shines brighter through the heavenly place.

They are praising Him in the dawning
   Of the endless, cloudless Day ;
But the songs of praise they used to sing
   Have died on the hills away ;—
Not half of all His beauty
   Was known to their hearts till now,
And new songs rise to the angel-lips
   For the new crowns on His brow.
But let all the *earth* keep silence
   Before the Lord to-day ;—
How would it be were sounds of woe
   To go up to His heart, through all the glow,
   From the shadows chill and gray ?

Trouble Him not in the dawning
   Of His bright, eternal Day ;
The days of His mourning are ended,
   And the last cloud passed away.

The morning shadows were sad and sweet
On the face of the little Child;
The evening shadows were black with
    wrath
On the worn Man undefiled,
And the clouds of Death have crossed the
    face
Uplifted now in the heavenly place,—
    But here in the golden Dawning,
        When the smiles of God appear,
    Let no man trouble the Master
        With mournful prayer or tear.

Yet,—come to Him in the dawning
    Of His bright, eternal Day:
He bendeth low from His holy Hill—
Searching the shadows gray and chill—-
    And calling to us alway;
And clear, through the angel-singing,—
    What time the Sons of God
Shout loud, for joy upspringing,
    Till all the heavens are bowed,—
He hears the faintest sighing
    Of some poor, far-off soul,
Who turns to look to the holy place
    While the billows round him rolL

And whenever, across the mountains
  That compass the City of God,
Some ransomed soul from earth set free
Draws near in robes of victory
  Unto the King's abode,
HE hears the far-off footstep
  Upon the hills of myrrh,
Through the sound of the living fountains
  And the sweet wind's wandering stir;
And He riseth up to greet
The trembling, joyful feet.

O glorious, tender Shepherd!
  On the far-off hills of God,
We will not fear to call to Thee,
Though hoarse and faint our voices be
  As they pass from cloud to cloud.
Let all men seek the Master;
  For, though the tempests roll,
Each tearful, upward gaze must meet
The Shepherd's look, which bendeth sweet
  On every seeking soul.

THE DESIRE TO DEPART.

"Hadad said unto Pharaoh, Let me depart, that I may go to mine own country. Then Pharaoh said unto him, But what hast thou lacked with me, that, behold, thou seekest to go to thine own country? And he answered, Nothing : howbeit let me go in any wise."—1 KINGS xi. 21, 22.

ND thus our hearts appeal to them,
    When we behold our dearest rise,
And look towards Jerusalem
    With strangely kindling eyes.

And thus we vainly seek to hide
    With the poor curtain of our love
The shining Gates that open wide,
    To welcome our sweet saints above.

Yet still to them, from that bright Land,
    Through our thin tent the Glory gleams;
Already lost to us they stand
    Wrapped in a mist of golden dreams:

For ah! the Master is so fair,
    His smile so sweet to banished men,
That they who meet it unaware
    Can never rest on Earth again.

And they who see Him risen afar
    At God's right hand to welcome them,
Forgetful stand of home and land,
    Desiring fair Jerusalem.

Yet had we lavished at their feet
    The precious ointment of hearts that break
For love; we counted sorrow sweet,
    And pain a crown for their dear sake:

"What have ye lacked, beloved, with us,"
    We murmur heavily and low,
"That ye should rise with kindling eyes,
    And be so fain to go?"

And tenderly the answer falls
    From lips that wear the smile of Heaven:
"Dear ones," they say, "we pass this day
    To Him by whom your love was given;

And in His Presence clear and true,
  We answer you with hearts that glow,—
No good thing have we lacked with you—
  Howbeit, let us go !"

And even as they speak, their thoughts
  Are wandering upward to the Throne.
Ah! God, we see, at length, how free
  All earthly ties must leave Thine own.

Yet, kneeling low in darkened homes,
  And weeping for the treasure spent,
We bless Thee, Lord, for that sweet word
  Our dear ones murmured as they went,—

It was not that our love was cold,
  That earthly lights were burning dim,
But that the Shepherd from His Fold
  Had smiled, and drawn them unto Him :

Praise God the Shepherd *is* so sweet !
  Praise God the Country *is* so fair !—
We could not hold them from His feet,—-
  We can but haste to meet them There

A PARABLE OF HOPE.

" And, lo, God hath given thee all them that sail with thee."—ACTS xxvii. 24

I.

OUT on a radiant sunlit Sea,
  Where the waves are leaping joyfully,
  And the breeze is blowing glad and free,
  We sail to the Land where we would be:
      We sail, and sing
      To the Unseen King,
  Whose smile on the Sea falls glittering.

And sailing, singing, over the Sea,
We dream of the Land where we would be;
And picture the Haven, fair and wide,
Where the longing heart shall be satisfied—
      And the face of One
      Who shines as the sun
In the kingdom which His sorrows won.

And fondly we pray that, tenderly thus,
God may guide the souls that sail with us—
That our Belovèd may also come
To the golden shore of the far-off Home:
  For Love will pray,
  Through her own bright day,
With a restless yearning that none can stay:—

" He leadeth me over the sleeping Sea,
 To the Home of the heart, where I would be;
But dearer souls than my own to me
Pass hither and thither carelessly:
  To and fro
  The bright sails go,
To the sounds of music tender and low.

" No thought of the Haven calm and fair,
No dream of the Master waiting there;
But a common sunshine upon the Sea,
And a breeze from the Land that bloweth free,
  Call forth the song,
  As they sail along,
From hearts so careless, and glad, and strong.

" So bright when the sun is shining sweet,
So brave when the waves and thunders meet,

Shall they miss the Haven fair and wide?
And shall I be there, well satisfied?
  Sweet Master, lean
  From Thy throne serene,
And call them to seek the Land Unseen."

Over a radiant sunlit Sea,
Where the waves are leaping joyfully,
And the breeze is blowing glad and free,
We sail to the Land where we would be;
  But Love must pray,
  Through her own bright day,
With a restless longing that none may stay,
For the names that dwell in her heart alway.

II.

Out on a wild and mournful Sea,
Where the waters are struggling heavily—
Where the sorrows of death are pressing nigh,
As the lights go out in the awful sky—
We wrestle against the wind and tide,
We wrestle in anguish, storm-defied.
  For the sake of a Land
  Whose shining sand
No eye hath seen—for the fame of a Sun
That never hath lightened earth or sea—

We wrestle and toil in agony :
No rest on the bitter driving Sea—
 No gleam in the closed and darkened Heaven ;
And days and nights that heavily
 Pass over the spirits tempest-driven.
Ah, who shall struggle and hope to the last ?
And who shall live when the storm is past ?

Yet out on the bitter driving Sea
In the hour of our own extremity,
Hear us, sweet Master, cry to Thee
For other souls which might sink or flee ;
  For Love must pray
  Through her own dark day
That light may shine on her loved alway.

" I struggle across the angry Sea
To the Home of the heart where I would be ;
Let me enter the Haven calm and fair,
But let my Belovèd be also there !
  One by one
  Let them greet the Sun
In the far-off Land which Thy sorrows won."

Ah, Lord, dear Master, who lovest well,
Thou knowest that angry storms may swell ;

That the great sea-billows may rise and roll,
But cannot drown Love: for still the soul
  From the wildest sea
  Will call to Thee,
" Save, Master, the souls that sail with me."

III.

Out on a changed and shadowy Sea,
Where the waters are heaving fitfully,
As we near the Haven where we would be,
When a new strange Light is dawning pale
On the moaning Sea, and the riven sail—
A Light that is neither of moon nor sun,
That ariseth cold, and fair, and sweet
On the shadowy Sea, when Night is done,
  And the golden Land
  So close at hand
Sends forth its fragrance our hearts to greet—

At that dim mysterious Hour of Peace,
That Dawn of death in which tears must
  cease,
Ere we pass from the faintly moaning Sea
To the Haven that shineth glad and free,
Still Love will pray from the shadowy Sea,
" Save, Master, the souls that sail with me !"

14

And the Lord will hear
In His kingdom near,
And send her a word of hope and cheer.

He giveth us peace at the last, they say,
And *more* than all for which Love can pray:
Will He send a sweet Angel to say to me,—
" Go in peace, to the Land of the joyful and free
For God hath given this day to thee
The souls thou hast prayed for steadfastly ?

" Go in peace, this day, to the Haven wide;
Thou shalt see His Face, and be satisfied;
Thou shalt know His heart, and rest in Him
With a peace which passeth thy knowledge dim :
Not for thyself alone, but for all
Thy heart hath yearned for, great and small.

" And some shall enter the Haven wide,
Full-sail, on the breast of a glorious tide;
And some shall come
To our golden Home
Sore battered and spent from an angry sea;
But thine heart shall count them, one by one,
And leap for joy as they greet the Sun,
Till God has gathered them all to thee."

MY WELL.*

" He that drinketh of this water shall thirst again."

I.

IN the wood, where the dreamy shadows
With dreamier sunbeams play,
Where the breezes whisper softly
Through the long summer day,
Secret, and cool, and musical,
My sweet Well lay.

The Well was deep, and the water,
From some mysterious spring,
Was ever gushing far below
With a tender murmuring ;
And, deep underground, a tiny rill
Stole on in the dark to sing.

* By the " Well" is here intended some innocent source of deep joy ; such
as the beauty and mystery of Nature, or the heart-thrilling power of Music, or
converse with a beloved friend, or the pursuit of some favourite study ; in
which our eyes may see depths of wonder, and ever-growing beauty, which we
cannot show to another.

This was my cherished Fountain,
　My Well of secret joy ;
Its beauty to me was perfect,
　Its peace had no alloy ;
I thought the weariest heart might there
　Sing like the heart of a boy.

When toiling afar in the City,
　Under a burning sky,
The very thought of my Well would come
　Like a Blessing from on High—
Like the voice of flowing waters,
　In a desert hot and dry.

One hour in the fragrant twilight,
　Of leaning over the Well,
While the hush of the forest touched my heart,
　To thought too sweet to tell,
And the music of the waters
　Wound me in a tender spell,—

One hour—and the heat and burden
　Of all the weary day
Were gone from me like the heavy dreams
　That flit with the Dawn away,
And my heart became like a little child
　That sings for joy alway.

As my spring-time melted sweetly
  Into the summer days,
I would sit by the Well till the evening star
  Dropped her sweet looks of praise
Into the secret waters,
  That trembled beneath her gaze ;

Then sweeter arose the music
  Of the waters crystal fair,
More heavenly for the silver star
  That had dropped and melted there,
And deeper grew the forest-trance
  As with the hush of prayer :

I drew of the silvered waters,
  I saw them glance and shine ;
And when I drank of the sparkling cup,
  Was it some spell divine,
Or something in mine own heart, that changed
  The water into wine ?

Then woke new life within me,
  Bounding as if from sleep ;
For my angel's hand had swept the chords,
  That only he can sweep,
Till the thunder rolled along my soul.
  Deep calling unto deep.

II.

There was one who passed through the Forest
　　At the close of a sultry day,
With a weary face and bleeding feet
　　That had trod a thorny way,—
My joy had taught me to pity pain,
　　And I called her where I lay ;

Where I lay by the mossy Fountain,
　　And heard in a heavenly dream
The low sweet play of the waters,
　　Which to my heart did seem
As dear as to God's bright Angels
　　The voice of the Eternal Stream !

' Dear heart, thou hast nothing to draw with,"
　　I said, " and the Well is deep ;
But thou shalt drink of my cup this day,
　　And thine eyes forget to weep,"—
And I offered the precious water
　　That should make the sad heart leap.

She drank of the crystal goblet,
　　And I watched the weary eyes,

But saw no hint of a glorious Dawn
   In their strange darkness rise,—
To her it was common water,
   Not wine of Paradise !

With sad thanks, dropping slowly
   From lips uncomforted,
She passed from me through the Forest gloom,
   Weary and hard bestead ;
And a low wind rose as she passed away,
   And sighingly I said :

The Well that to me is a Fountain,
   Mystical and Divine,
To other men is a common Well
   Where earthly waters shine ;
Henceforth shall no stranger meddle
   With the joy that is only mine !

III.

As the low wind died in the Forest
   From my heart the shadow fell ;
I kissed the crystal goblet,
   To seal once more its spell,—
When I was aware of a Stranger
   Who sat beside the Well.

The golden arrows of sunset
　　Gleamed on the shadowy grass ;
And, bending over the waters,
　　I saw an image pass—
A face like the face of an Angel,
　　Darkly as in a glass.

My heart stood still, and the twilight
　　Suddenly deepened round ;
The low sad wind of the Forest
　　Came back with a sighing sound,
And stirred the stately trees, which bent
　　Solemnly toward the ground.

And a Voice beside me, falling
　　Softly as summer rain
Into my heart, awoke it
　　To a yearning hope and pain,—
" He that drinketh of these bright waters
　　Shall thirst again."

I turned and met the look
　　Of One most sweet ;—
I read the signs of the Master,
　　And fell at His wounded feet ;
I poured out my soul in weeping,
　　And Earth and Heaven did meet.

" I have waited for thee," He murmured,
 " Through weary nights and days,
Beside the Well in the twilight,
 And along thy devious ways—
But thou wert content to miss Me ;"
 And I met His tender gaze.

' Content no more, sweet Master,
 Except Thou be with me,
From this time forth, in the City,
 Where my daily toil must be ;
And at evening-time by the Fountain,
 Where I will sing to Thee !"

He raised me up and kissed me,
 That sweet yet awful Priest,—
He gave me the Cup of Blessing
 From the Eternal Feast,
The wine with hues more radiant
 Than sunrise in the East :

That moment, beside my Fountain,
 I heard, as if in a dream,
The low sweet play of the waters,
 Which to pause and fail did seem ;
And I trembled to hear the falter
 In the music's silver stream.

I looked in the Face of the Master,
   For strength to let it go :—
"The Fountain *changeth* its music,"
   He answered, " and falleth low ;
But its voice shall ever be sweet to thee,
   And ever its waters flow."

And I knew at length, that, if only
   We give Him His royal seat,
The earthly music will take its place,
   And tremble around His feet,—
Sweeter than ever, because to our heart
   The Master is still more sweet !

Then glowed in the skies above me
   Bright stars I had not seen ;
They shone on the face of the Master
   Glorious and serene ;—
When I meet Him again, beyond the stars,
   Will the ecstasy be more keen ?

IV.

The shadows were black and awful,
   The midnight wind was high,
As I sought through the moaning Forest
   For one who was ready to die.

Till I found her, wounded and fainting,
    And raised her tenderly :

" Dear heart, I have found the Master ;
    He is sweet beyond compare :
He will save and comfort thy weary soul,
    He will make thee white and fair ;
Not as I gave thee, will *He* give,
    But wine Divine and rare !"

She drank of the Cup of Blessing
    From the Eternal Feast,
The Wine whose hues are radiant
    As sunrise in the East ;
Then with a smile she fell asleep,
    Upon the Master's breast.

    *   *   *   *

He is with me in the tumult
    Of the City harsh and dim,
And at evening by the Fountain,
    Where I sit and sing to Him ;—
Now He wears a veil of shadows
    On the Face Divine and fair,
But His Angels whisper to me
    " There will be no shadows There !"

AFTER THE BATTLE.

Y wound is deep, I fain would sleep ; O Lord,
I stretch my hands to Thee :
Do Thou according to Thy faithful word,
And set Thy servant free !

Sore hath the battle been, but Victory
Crowned me as evening fell ;
Now heart and flesh are failing, let me see
The land where I would dwell.

The Battle-field is cold and silent now,
Its thunders sunk to rest ;
And I can feel the touch upon my brow
Of low winds from the West :

The clouds of sleep, the last and longest sleep,
Are heavy on mine eyes ;
They cannot watch, dear Lord, they cannot weep
Beneath Thy dark'ning skies.

What time the Angel, Victory, came down
   To bid my conflict cease,
And crowned my tired soul with the shining
     crown
   Of Righteousness and Peace,

That instant broke the sound as of a knell
   On the faint evening's breath ;
And on my parched mouth, like the dew, there
     fell
   The soft sweet kiss of Death :

For Victory and Death walk hand in hand
   Down all the Battle-field—
One ruddy as the Dawn, the other grand,
   But pale behind his shield ;

And whom God loves, to whom is victory
   On such a field as this,
Receive the radiant Angel's crown, and see
   The pale cold Angel's kiss :

That kiss has made my spirit faint and weak ;
   Lord, take me to thy breast ;
Oh, fold me closely, where the weariest seek
   And find Eternal Rest !

Christ, who has been my perfect sun by day,
   Will be my star by night ;
On my deep rest the Lord shall shine alway,
   An everlasting Light.

Dimly I see him, through the clouds that roll
   Along the dark'ning West:
O Lord, my Star, by Thy sweet light my soul
   Doth enter into Rest.

FROM DEATH TO LIFE.

" It grieved Him at His heart."
" Then said I, Lo, I come."

VER against His Dead
    God sat in silence : for the Earth was dead,
    And dimly lay upon her awful bier,
    Wrapped round in darkness; yea, her shroud
        was wrought
Of clouds and thunders : for the Earth had died,
Not gently and at peace, as tired men die
Toward the evening ; but as one who dies
Full of great strength, by sudden smiting down.
The Earth was dead, and laid upon her bier,
And God, Sole Mourner, watched her day and
    night—
The living God a Watcher by the dead,
Sole Mourner in the Universe for her
Who had been once so fair.   The Angels sang
As sweetly that sad night when she lay dead,
As they had sung the morning of her birth.

They sang aloud for joy, though one lay dead
In that low House which stood so far beneath
Their golden heights, with clouds and stars between
They knew no funeral march, no song of Death ;
They sang of Life and Glory, and the Sea
Of Glass, with all its bright waves, echoed back
Their voices to the starry shores of Heaven.
Sole Mourner, for in the dark outer Room
The Devils danced and sang for dreary joy,
Because God's so beloved Earth was dead,
And must be shortly buried out of sight
To perish.
    Still,—over against His Dead
God sat in silence.
      But, behold, there came
One, treading softly to the House of Death,
Down from among the Angels, through the room.
He came, as comes a King, unto the place
Where lay the Dead ; and He laid His right hand
Of strength on her, and called her tenderly,
Saying, " Arise, beloved, from thy sleep,
For I will ransom thee by Death to Life ;
Arise and live."   And He did raise her up
By His right hand, presenting her to God,
All glorious, as one who hath been dead
But hath found life and immortality,

And God, the Mighty God, did there rejoice,
And rest in His great love ; for this His Earth,
Which had been dead, was living in His sight.
Therefore He crowned with many crowns His head
Who had prevailed to ransom her from Death ;
And also, laying joy upon *her* head
For everlasting, He hath made her Bride
Of Christ, the King.

"BEHOLD THE MAN."

I.—"NO BEAUTY IN HIM."

E told me I am blind,
    As well as lame: I think it must be true;
    For I have striven in vain to see the Light
    Which dawns, they say, on Israel's dreary
       night
Sweetly as on Mount Hermon falls the dew.
I sit by the way-side, and they pass by
Who company with Him. I sometimes try
To raise myself a little; sometimes cry,
"Will no man lift me by the hand, and show
The Christ to me, who cannot rise and go?"
And once, some one stepped from the busy crowd,
Saying, "Arise ! behold, He draweth nigh !
Arise, and look upon the face of God !
The Man that is His image passeth by !
Behold the Man ! His glory passeth by !"

He stooped to me, and, holding by the hand
This man who loved HIM, I could rise and stand.
The sun was hot upon the thirsty land ;
The very leaves were hot upon the trees,
And cast no coolness on the dusty road ;
And, lo ! a Man passed by : to whom the crowd
Did look with eager eyes, and follow close ;
And in the burning heat of those noon-rays
They seemed to feel no burden, so His face
In journeying were lifted up on them.
So passed they on, towards Jerusalem.
And I was left behind : and unto him
Who stood by me with rapt and earnest gaze
Which followed after Him, and seemed to trace
With loving care the very footprints dim,
I said, "Is *this* the man ? I see no God
Shine manifest in Him. As He passed by,
The sun was never shadowed on the way,
But smote His face as boldly with its ray
As yours or mine. He seemed a patient man,
And somewhat worn with toil, and one may read,
With some sore work before Him, which may lay
A heavier weight on that now bended head.
I saw no beauty in Him." Thus I said.
He never answered me ; he only stood,
Still gazing up the hill, by the hot road

Where they had passed. I think that he heard
   still
The footsteps of the Man he loved so well.
And, as he listened, my dim eyes could see
That, ever bright'ning, shone the smile of peace
More sweetly on his face than falls the smile
Of moonlight on the waves of Galilee.
Surely the memory will never cease
To thrill me ; for I felt that I could see
In that sweet joy upon His servant's face,
Reflected, the fair light I failed to see
Upon the face of Christ, as He passed by.
I trembled at that joy and love, for I
Had found no share.   I gave a bitter cry
Of sudden fear—" *Was* there some glory there ?
Oh ! would to God that I had seen it then !"
He turned to me, at that sharp cry of pain—
" Some glory ! oh," he said, " this noon-day blaze
Is cold and white by reason of His face,
Which shineth as the light of seven days ;
And all sweet things are bitter to His smile,
Which is more sweet than the sweet stars of God.
Oh, thou art blind," he said, " as I, erewhile !
Arise, and come with me along the road,
And let us follow Him.   I cannot stay
Away from Him : I think He calleth me

Over the mountains.   Is not that the sound
Of my Beloved's voice ?   I cannot stay ;
We will go on.   Rise up, and come away !"
But I made answer, " Lo, the mid-day sun
Is hot upon the hills ; and I am lame,
And weakened in the way : I cannot go ;
What little strength I had is well-nigh spent :
I cannot go."   And he rose up and went
With eager eyes unto the silent hills.
He went to Christ, and I sit here alone—
Alone by the road-side.   The afternoon
Grows cold ; but I've no heart to rise and creep
To my poor home across the dark'ning hill ;
I rather sit by the road-side and weep.
I think there *must* have been some glory still.
Oh, would to God that I had seen it then !
I sit and think of this with bitter pain,
In the deep shadows and the falling dew,
As the night falls.   He told me I am blind,
As well as lame : I think it must be true.

II.—" ALTOGETHER LOVELY."

The hot day dies upon the dreary hill,
And the cold winds of night arise, and creep
Across the valleys, and I sit and weep
Alone by the road-side, and cheerless still.

The winds are rising, and a sudden blast
Of bitter rain drives sharply through the air ;
And in the angry sky the clouds toss fast,
Wild, broken, white with moonlight here and there
And in the white light of that stormy moon
On the far hill-side I have caught the form
Of One who cometh, and will reach me soon.
Through the cold moonlight and the windy storm,
Over the stony mountain-track He comes
With slow and weary steps, until He stands
Close at my side, and lifteth up His hands,
As if He had been an Anointed Priest,
To bless me.   And, behold, it was the Man
Who passed that way at noon-day in the sun !
I did not say, " No glory" *now*, although
His face was paler, with the busy day
Spent since at noon-tide He had passed that way:
And with the flitting rays of that white moon
(Which was so bright that I could see each stone
Upon the mountain-road), on that pale face
I saw the cloud of Godhead rest, and knelt.

*   *   *   *   *

Then He sat down beside me; made me lean
My head upon His shoulder, while the keen
North wind blew still across the dreary hills,

With sudden blasts of bitter rain, and then
White moonbeams falling on our heads between.
My head upon His shoulder! Oh, the thrill
Of joy and trembling sweeping through my heart,
Which no wild winds of earth could check or chill.
But with it came the memory of that word
Spoken long since in vision, of the Lord,
That they should name Him "Wonderful," and on
His shoulder should the Government be laid:
This shoulder where I laid my weary head!
And then I trembled; but His strong right hand
Upheld me, and His left hand's kind embrace
Brought back to me that other sacred word,
Foretelling Him as Shepherd, who should stand
And feed the flock of God, and often place
The lambs upon His shoulder tenderly;
Then I rejoiced, and rested on the Lord.
And then He turned, and said unto the bright
And stormy moonlit night, " Oh, peace, be still,"
(Not for His own sake, though the drops of night
Were heavy in His hair, and from the hill
Above us, where the lonely palm-tree stands,
The winds blew on His cold pale cheek and hands).
And, with the kingly words, the angry, dim,
Wild clouds swept back; the wings of the great
     winds

Were folded straightway, as they crouched to Him
And the soft moon shone cloudlessly and sweet,
And weaving fast her silver rays in crowns,
Cast them upon the ground before His feet.
So, 'mid these silent, moonlit hills alone,
The angels saw us through the long still night;
We heard afar the Jordan's heavy moan,
And on the western hill the road shone white
Which leadeth on towards Jerusalem.
And in the calm He spake great words to me
Regarding God, and sin, and Love Divine,
Which should be manifest, and of a Death
He must accomplish shortly, for the sin
Of many;—He, Himself, whose living breath
Gives life to all the nations; yea, the Man
Who is the Fellow of Almighty God.
And often I could see He turned His face
Westward unto Jerusalem.   The road
Over the hills was gleaming in the moon,
And sometimes suddenly it seemed there shone
A Light that was not moonlight on the road;
It might be angels passing, bright, yet dim—
I cannot tell, I only thought of Him.
So went the night.   At length the first cold gleam
Of dawn crept silently, like some pale dream,
Along the eastern hills; and the first cold

Faint breath of morning quivered in the trees.
Then He who communed with me lifted up
His eyes unto the hills, and said, " Behold,
The day is breaking." And again He said,
—For I was clinging to Him—" Let Me go,
For the day breaketh." But I held Him so
As when a drowning man holds on for life :
"I cannot let Thee go, dear Lord, dear Lord,
Except thou bless me: leave me some good word
Oh, tarry with me. Leave me not alone
And comfortless, lest I should die, undone !"
" I will not leave thee comfortless," He said,
" For I will come to thee;" and on my head
He laid his hands, and blessed me audibly,
—With full forgiveness for all my sin,
—With victory, which He, not I, should win,
And with exceeding great and precious words
Of promise. (And, behold, in that same hour
I felt a thrill of health, with sudden power,
Shoot through my weary, wasted frame, and stood
A crippled man in Israel no more.)
" And thou shalt see My face, what time thy feet
Stand safe within the Holy City gate."
So spake He; but He lifted not his eyes
Towards *thy* gates, mine own Jerusalem !
But as He spoke, He looked to those faint skies

Which swept, so dream-like, over Him and me,
Unto some pearly Gates which *He* could see—
Not I—beyond the dawning.

*   *   *   *   *   *

I often think of that strange moonlight night
On the Judean hills; and while I work
His work who saved me, I lift up mine eyes
Unto the higher Hills, where I shall stand
What time the years are done, and meet with Him
He hath accomplished now that sacrifice
Whereof He spake to me, and in the land
Of God He reigneth Conqueror and King.
And I shall see His face, what time my feet
Stand safe upon the Holy City street.

IN MEMORIAM.—PROFESSOR MILLER.

DIED JUNE 17, 1864

" He calleth to me out of Seir, Watchman, what of the night? Watchman, what of the night? The watchman said, The Day cometh, and also the night."

" HAT of the night?
   Great Watchman of the House of Israel,
      Who holdest forth the Light,
   And, slumbering not, art watching on the
      Hill
Through all the ages ; answer from the Height,
      What of the night?

      " What of the night?
Dear Lord, I seek a double boon from Thee ;—
      I seek the light
Of God's fair Dawn, my soul from shadows free
But for my weary hands and failing sight
      I seek a Night.

"What of the night?
I would be patient—I will work and wait,
 Thy stars are bright ;
But in the End, when watching hours grow late,
I pray not only, Lord, let there be Light,--
 Let there be Night.

"What of the night?
I stand upon the shore of the great Sea,
 And my dim light
Is flickering in the night-wind ;—answer me,
Watchman above me on the distant Height,
 What of the night ?"

"*This* of the night,
Tired Pilgrim through the shadows and the mist,
 There shall be Light ;
The fair Dawn cometh shortly up the East :
—Also, for toil-worn hands and failing sight,
 There shall be Night."

 *   *   *   *   *

It *is* the Night :
The Pilgrim lays him down at last to rest
 Among the lilies white ;

Rest for the toil-worn hands and anxious breast,
In those dim shadows underneath the Height,
    In the still Night.

    It is the Night ;
He sleepeth well beneath those soft gray skies
    After the fight :
The Night is come upon him, and he lies
Wrapped closely from all earthly sound or sight
    In God's still Night.

    It is the Night,
And God has given His Beloved sleep :
    The stars are bright,
And, as he lieth in those shadows deep,
The Watchman bendeth o'er him from the Height
    And guards his Night.

*   *   *   *   *

    It is the *Day;*
The Pilgrim gets him up unto the Height,—
    All shadows fled away—
To the broad sunshine of Eternal Light,
Unto the face of God, which shines alway
    In the glad Day.

It is the Day;
No more sad watchings by the midnight Sea,
—No twilight gray,
But, crowned with light and immortality,
He stands from henceforth, triumphing alway
In God's own Day.

THE WAKING HEART.

" I sleep, but my heart waketh."

T is the Night; the lights are burning low,
  The house is still,
And through the heavy chambers come and
  go,
  At their own wayward will,
The Dreams that thrill the Night, with murmurings
Of voices, mingled with a rush of wings.

And going through the house, we are aware
  Of Dreams upon the wall,
Of Visions passing up the shadowy stair,
  And through the vacant hall;
And every sleeper, in his darkened room,
Is busy with his guests, in joy or gloom.

Ah! calm and still may be the sleeping face
  In the moonlight pale,

But the heart waketh in her secret place,
    Within the veil ;
And agonies are suffered in the Night,
Or joys embraced, too keen for waking sight.

A cold wind blows out of the starry North,—
    Strange Doors stand wide,—
And hidden things, and things long past, come forth
    And will not be denied,
Though some be terrible and sad to face,—
And the Heart mourneth, stricken, in her place.

But still she *wakes;* and, steadfast, will not turn
    To seek for rest ;—
All the long Night her faithful Lamp will burn,
    In the clear breast,
Where Angels come and go, to minister
God's consolations, tenderly, to her.

Then come dear living ones across the Sea,
    From distant lands,—
Then come her Holy Dead, in ecstasy,
    With lilies in their hands,—
And looks, more sweet to these poor hearts of ours
Than even that fragrance of Eternal flowers !

And, dearer than the living ones, that dwell
    Beyond the throbbing Sea,—
And, dearer than the Dead, whose voices swell
    The Heavenly melody,—
ONE visiteth His people in the Night,
Who giveth songs, and makes the darkness bright.

"I sleep; yet evermore my Heart doth wake,
    Within the veil;
The voice of my Beloved! hear it break
    Across the moonlight pale:
He is come down to comfort me awhile,
And cheer the sad Night with His tender smile!"

   *   *   *   *   *

And when the days and nights of Earth are flown,
    And I lie dead,
Then come and write, dear friends, upon the stone
    Above my quiet head,—
"I sleep;—yet far, upon the Crystal Sea,
    My Heart is waking,—waking, Lord, with
    Thee!"

For I shall sleep beneath the steadfast sky,
    So free from care,
That evermore my hands may folded lie,
    As if in prayer;

16

And evermore the sealèd eyelids keep
The secret of dim eyes, that, joyful, sleep:

And, whilst I sleep, behold! my Heart will wake,
    And sing its perfect song,
In thy sweet Presence, Master, for whose sake
    It watched and waited long;
And evermore Thy deathless Love shall be
The treasure of the Heart that loveth Thee!

IN THE MIDST.*

HUNDRED lights are gleaming on the throng
Of radiant faces passing to and fro ;
And on gay robes, and flowers, and sparkling
gems ;
And pictures on the wall, where Southern suns
Glow strangely rich and bright—fair suns, which rose
And set in glory far beyond the Sea,
Here prisoned for our pleasure, that so our night
May borrow beauty from their vanished days.
And men are here, whose names are written great
In the World's Book of Life ; and women, fair
As any summer dawn.   On every face
The light of innocent mirth, in every voice
Something of laughter ; for the cares of life
Are laid down for an hour, and all can smile.

* At a recent gay public Reception, where the pictures gathered were very
fine, there was one which must have appealed to many hearts—a picture of the
Christ, as a King, " treading the Winepress alone."

Now the sweet tide of Music, rising, flows
In countless waves upon the radiant air,
Fast quick'ning every heart to fuller life :
It touches every picture, every face,
To a fresh brightness ; by its help I read
New meanings in these visions on the wall—
More of the heart's light in each changing face—
And even a fairer beauty in the flowers,
As the soft music breathes and blows on them,
Like some rare wandering wind from Paradise ;—
And the lights gleam more gaily over all.

And suddenly face to face with Him I stood
Who is not very far at any time
From those who love Him, yet who seemed afar
And lonely in the midst of us that night.
We had the hundred lights ; but He in the dark,
Treading a darker Winepress, stood before
My startled sight.   A crown was on His brow,
— And all His air was lofty, like a king's ;
ʃ But measureless pain and grief had hold on Him—
His eyes were sorrowful even unto death.
And thus He faced us : He for us alone
Treading the Winepress ; whilst we came and went
With songs and flowers beneath our hundred lights,
As if we knew Him not.

Had it been He
Sitting in cheerful friendliness, as once
At the marriage-feast in Cana, giving them,
From His own royal bounty, wine and joy
And all things, it had seemed less strange to me ;
And we, in all our innocent mirth, not far,
Not very far, from Him. But here, alone,
Treading the mystical Winepress full of woe,
In the last Passion of His agony,
He stood amongst us on our festal night.
Alone, O Christ !—yea, evermore alone
In that strange anguish, even when close to Thee
Thy people press with tears : a little light
Must still be with us, dear hands clasping ours,
When pale we stand before Thy lifted Cross,
And see Thee hang, forsaken, in the dark.
Then *now* alone that hour, that glittering hour,
When suddenly face to face with Thee I stood,
And no man wept for Thee.   We came and went
As gaily as the music ; and the sound
Of soft, low laughter came and went with us.

And now, sweet Master, when my heart is gay,
And the rich music of my happy life
Sounds on and falters not—when dear ones press
With loving faces round me, and the light

Is almost like the light of seven days—
Let something of that pictured vision rise
Often before my face.   So shall I keep
For ever in my heart one silent space ;
A little sacred spot of loneliness,
Where to set up the memory of Thy Cross—
A little quiet garden, where no man
May pass or rest for ever, sacred still
To visions of Thy Sorrow and Thy Love.

HYMN

SUNG AT THE OPENING OF ALL SAINTS' CHURCH,
CHESTER.

" Lift up your heads, O ye gates, and the King of Glory shall come in."

COME, to bless Thy people, Lord,
    From the hills of peace afar ;
    Come, and let Thy whispered word
    Greet the souls that weary are.
Lo ! Thy congregation waits
One sweet look from Thee to win :
Lift your heads on high, ye gates—
Christ, our King, will enter in.

Come, and let Thy glory dwell
    In this house for evermore,
Great High Priest of Israel,
    Whom the Saints in light adore.

He has heard our prayer—He waits
　　To absolve us from all sin :
Lift your heads on high, ye gates—
　　Christ, our Priest, will enter in.

Signs of sorrow never cease
　　In a world so stained with guilt ;
And where'er a house of peace
　　For the Prince of Peace is built,
Lo ! a congregation waits,
　　Sorely pressed by toil and sin :
Lift your heads on high, ye gates—
　　Let the mourners enter in.

We will bid the poor, to meet
　　In this house our promised Guest ;
We will lead them to the Feet
　　Where the weary are at rest ;
For them all His mercy waits,
　　Smiles and blessings they shall win :
Lift your heads on high, ye gates,
　　That Christ's poor may enter in.

Who are we, to entertain,
　　In the house our hands have made,
Him, the glory of whose train
　　Makes the stainless Heavens afraid ?

Yet He comes, and sweetly waits
  Entrance to our hearts to win :
Lift your heads on high, ye gates—
  Let the gentle Master in.

And as *we* receive this day
  Joyfully our Royal Guest,
So at length, when far away,
  Breaks the dawn of promised rest.
Where the Lord His Church awaits,
  Sweetest welcome may we win :
" Lift your heads, ye golden gates—
  Let My ransomed people in ! "
    Amen.

www.ingramcontent.com/pod-product-compliance
Lightning Source LLC
Chambersburg PA
CBHW030813020726
47499CB00006B/1899